escaping
into the
night

D. Dina Friedman

Simon & Schuster Books for Young Readers
New York London Toronto Sydney

SIMON & SCHUSTER BOOKS FOR YOUNG READERS

An imprint of Simon & Schuster Children's Publishing Division

1230 Avenue of the Americas, New York, New York 10020

SIMON & SCHUSTER BOOKS FOR YOUNG READERS is a trademark of Simon & Schuster, Inc.

Book design by Christopher Grassi

The text for this book is set in Adobe Jansen.

Manufactured in the United States of America

10 9 8 7 6 5 4 3 2 1

Library of Congress Cataloging-in-Publication Data

Friedman, D. Dina.

Escaping into the night / D. Dina Friedman.—1st ed.

p. cm.

Summary: Thirteen-year-old Halina Rudowski narrowly escapes the Polish ghetto and flees to the forest, where she is taken in by an encampment of Jews trying to survive World War II.

ISBN-13: 978-1-4169-0258-4 (isbn 13)

ISBN-10: 1-4169-0258-9 (isbn 10)

1. Holocaust, Jewish (1939–1945)—Juvenile fiction. [1. Holocaust, Jewish (1939–1945)—Fiction. 2. World War, 1939–1945—Fiction.] I. Title.

PZ7.F896474Esc 2006

[Fic]—dc22

2005015768

For my husband, Shel Horowitz.
I couldn't have chosen a better life partner.

chapter
one

I could smell Mama's perfume when she woke me up. Georg must have gotten it for her on the black market. The scent was faint, and muted by cigarette smoke, but she smelled like Mama—dark, sweet, and smoky. "There's extra bread," she said, "and three whole potatoes we can make for supper. Georg brought them last night."

She didn't have to tell me he had been here. I'd heard them talking, all night and far into the morning. Like most of Mama's boyfriends, Georg only appeared sporadically, but at least he hadn't disappeared—yet. I hoped he cared for Mama more than the others did, even if he never had much to say to me. Still, I didn't like him too much; his wild plans really scared me.

I squinted at Mama from my bedroll on the dusty floor. "What if the Nazis heard what Georg said? What if they come here looking for him and arrest us?"

Mama inhaled on what was left of the nub of her cigarette. "It's just talk. You're such a worrier, Halina. Like your grandmother. 'Ikh hob moyre,' all she ever said was how worried she was." She clucked her tongue. "I thought I'd shielded you from that peasant mentality and here you are, like your grandmother's ghost."

I hated it when she said that to me. It wasn't as if we had nothing to worry about. And even if being thirteen meant I should act more grown up, it was too hard to pretend everything was fine when it wasn't. I was tired of pretending not to care when the guards hit someone with their rifles, tired of pretending not to hear gunshots in the streets. Wasn't thirteen the age when you were supposed to stop pretending?

I dressed for work, then grabbed a piece of black bread and sank my teeth into it, trying to chew as slowly as possible. Yesterday all I'd had to eat was one small, moldy potato.

"I just don't want the Nazis to torture us," I whispered.

"Nothing bad will happen—nothing worse than what we have already. Georg has a good position on the Jewish Police. He'll protect us." Mama drew me to her. She stroked my hair and I smelled her perfume again. She hadn't hugged me in a while, and I wanted to hold on to her for a long time, but in a second she pulled away. "You need to finish getting ready. We have to leave in five minutes."

Once we were outside, Mama walked ahead of me, assuming her blank, fade-into-the-scenery look. That was the safest way to be in the ghetto. When they first sent us to Poland, we went to her village, but a few months later, the Nazis came and made us move to Norwogrodek. They built a wall around the section where we lived and lined it with barbed wire. We couldn't leave the area without permission.

The narrow streets were filled with people. I watched two soldiers carting away a group of old women who were covered with sores. I tried not to look at others like them huddled in the doorways. I tried to hold my breath because they smelled so bad. I tried to pretend, to wipe the worry off my face and make it blank like Mama's, but it was hard, because I kept thinking about what I'd overheard last night. Georg said the Germans were going to have another selection. He wanted Mama to run away to the forest, but Mama said she wasn't cut out for that kind of life. "It's better to stay here," she insisted. "In your position you can protect us."

But Georg couldn't protect the Rojaks when Batya's brother, Yosl, was taken away last month. Batya, her father, and her other brothers who lived with us in our room prayed for days, but God didn't help either. They kept praying anyway—every morning and every night. I couldn't believe how religious they were.

The guard at the gate was the older man today, who always seemed sleepy and uninterested. But I still didn't hug Mama good-bye—it was too dangerous to show that you cared about somebody. Sometimes the guards made dirty remarks when we passed them, but other times Fritz was there. Fritz talked to me if no one was looking, because once he heard me humming, and we discovered that we both like to sing. Fritz sang in the opera before they recruited him into the army. He told me he couldn't wait for the war to be over so he could go back. He sang for me once. I had to keep walking and pretend he wasn't singing for me, but his voice was amazing. I think he could have cracked a glass.

Before the war my one wish would have been to sing as well as Fritz could. When we still lived in Germany, I practiced my singing every day; I even did all the boring warm-ups that Frau Schneider, my voice teacher, seemed to like so much, scales and arpeggios and breath control. Frau Schneider only gave me simple songs to learn, but after we saw *The Magic Flute*, Mama bought me the score and I secretly practiced all the arias. My favorite was the aria of the Queen of the Night. I knew Frau Schneider would say it was too hard for me, but I just loved the way it sounded so strong. Whenever I sang that aria, I felt transformed into someone magical and powerful. I was going to sing it for Frau Schneider after I'd made it perfect, but soon after I'd started to learn it, we had to leave Berlin. We left so quickly, I didn't even have time to tell Frau Schneider good-bye. We could barely take anything with us, not even my rock collection. I think Mama just said that because she never liked it when I brought rocks home and put them on all the windowsills. "No one knows where those rocks have been!" she'd say. Even after she washed them in hot water, she still said the rocks were dirty.

After we passed the gate, Mama and the Rojaks headed toward the munitions factory. I walked in the other direction toward the commander's wife's house, which I cleaned every day. When her husband wasn't around, the commander's wife was kind to me. Sometimes she told me about her life in a small city called Rostock. She had grown up near the beach, and she had a wonderful shell collection. When I told her about the rocks I had to leave behind, she told me I could take a shell from her, whatever shell I wanted. I picked a shell that looked like coral with little holes that reminded me of hiding places, and I put it on the windowsill, just as I had done with my rocks at home. When Mama saw it, she didn't insist on washing it, though she frowned when I told her who had given it to me. "Be careful," she said. "She might turn on you and say that you stole it from her."

That evening, the commander's wife gave me some chicken. It was so rich and I'd been so hungry for so long, I could barely eat it. I wanted to save some to share with Mama and the

Rojaks, but I didn't want to risk someone stealing it from me on the way home, so I ate as much as I could and thanked her, hoping she wouldn't be angry that I wasn't grateful enough to finish it all. She just smiled and patted me on the head. "I wish I had a daughter," she said. Then she looked away from me, out the window, and I knew it was time to leave.

The streets were quiet as I approached the ghetto gate. A light spring rain had begun to fall and the sound of it reminded me of an Italian song Frau Schneider had taught me. I bit my lip because whenever I thought of a song, I'd start to hum it out loud, and that could be dangerous if the guards were in a bad mood. I hoped Fritz would be at the gate. He wouldn't care. But it was the older man again. I handed him my papers and looked at the ground until he grunted. Then I moved on as quickly as I could. The Nazis didn't like us in the streets.

As usual, I stamped the ground hard when I opened the door to our building, hoping to scare the rats into hiding. Batya's father told me to imagine them receding into the walls like the parting of the Red Sea. I liked his stories, and the way he always tried to cheer me up when I was scared. I often wondered whether my father would have told me stories. He left us when I was a baby. All I had was a picture of a bald man with a bushy mustache. His name was Grisha Rudowski. Mama told me I was built like him, but she didn't seem happy to tell me that. He was a big, stocky peasant from Poland who met Mama in Berlin. When he lost his job and couldn't find work, he went back to his farm. Mama liked the city too much to go with him. I think the worst day for Mama was when the Nazis sent us back to Poland. Mama told me she had spent her whole life trying to find a way out of her little village. I think that was even worse for her than the day the Nazis moved us into the ghetto. Of course, we didn't know then how bad the ghetto could be.

The apartment was empty, exactly the way it had been when we left in the morning; Mama's cigarette butt was still lying on the cracked saucer, next to the torn movie magazine she had filched out of the garbage. I opened the cupboard to find something to eat, then remembered that I'd already had chicken, so I decided to make Georg's potatoes for Mama. I found the peeler, scraped off the skin and the mold, then put some water up to boil. The chimes rang in the main part of town. One more hour before curfew. Mama and the Rojaks were usually back by now. Had they all been held late at the factory? I looked out the window to see if they were on their way. No one was in sight.

I drained the water and covered the pot to keep the potatoes hot, then looked out the window again. A lone man, tall and gangly like a spider, hurried along the street. He sneaked into an alley as a guard passed, then inched out again, propelling from alleyway to alleyway in short bursts. I heard noise on the stairs. Mama at last! But the footsteps weren't Mama's. There was a knock on the door.

I froze.

We all knew that a knock on a door after dark could mean only one thing. The Nazis!

Could I pretend no one was here? They could probably smell the potatoes.

There was another knock, louder and more urgent.

"Halina!" The whisper was hoarse and raspy. "It's Georg. You must let me in!"

Mama's boyfriend pushed his way inside as soon as I undid the latch, then leaned against the wall, panting to catch his breath. His graying, curly hair drooped into his bloodshot eyes.

"Mama's not here."

"I know. She was taken. Everyone at the munitions factory is gone."

"Gone?"

The word hung in the air like a bad smell. I looked at the bare walls and down at my hands, which were rough and red from bleach. What was he saying? How could Mama be gone?

"What happened?"

"I don't know exactly."

"Is she . . ."

I felt a stillness inside, an emptiness, then a moment where it felt as if I couldn't breathe. And then a big breath, a big, sad wave with a sound louder than any sound I thought I could make forced its way out of me before I could stop it.

"Shh!" Georg clasped his hand over my mouth and drew me close to him. He smelled of sweat, mold, and garlic. "They're planning to empty the entire ghetto within the next three weeks," he whispered in my ear. "We must act quickly. Plans are in place. The escape route is almost complete. But we must bribe the right people. Your mother said she had money hidden in the cupboard."

"How can you think about money now?"

Had Georg ever really cared for Mama at all? It was his fault, all of it. The Nazis had found out what he was doing and were taking people away before they could escape. I clenched my fists and pounded at him, trying to wrench myself away. I wanted to hit him over and over until he brought Mama back.

"I came to help you, to help all of us." Georg's words were sharp as he grabbed my wrists. "Before it's too late."

It was already too late.

I shook myself free from his grasp and walked over to the window, looking for Mama one more time. The streets were empty. The commander's wife's coral lay gleaming on the sill. I picked it up and threw it down hard on the floor. It broke into small sharp pieces.

"I made the potatoes you brought for Mama," I said, still looking at the shards.

"Eat them. You need your strength."

"I can't. You may as well eat them."

Georg took the pot and began to stuff the potatoes into his mouth in large, quick forkfuls. I looked toward the door again. He had to be wrong. In just a few minutes Mama would come in the way she always did. She'd take off her shoes and massage her swollen feet. The Rojaks would come back too. Mr. Rojak and his sons would chant their evening prayers as Batya fixed them supper.

Georg rose and handed me the empty pot. "The Germans are planning to start the liquidation in three days," he said. "I don't like the idea of leaving you here alone, but I have work to do. Tonight we will put our plans in place. Tomorrow night we will go. Tomorrow you must go to your job as usual. You must act as if nothing has happened. Tomorrow night I will come for you." Georg opened the cupboard and took Mama's money out from under a small can of peas. "Wear as many clothes as you can. Anything you want to take must be small enough to fit inside your pockets."

If I still had my rock collection, I could have put some of the stones in my pockets, I thought. Not all of them, just a few of the ones I liked the best, the ones with flecks of mica that shone in the sunlight—my lucky stones.

"We're going to the forest," Georg said. "Believe me, it is the safest place."

"But what if Mama comes back?"

We both looked at the floor again, at the broken coral. I knew what he was thinking, what we both were thinking.

No one who had disappeared had ever come back.

Georg awkwardly patted my shoulder, then slipped out, closing the door behind him.

chapter
two

For a long time I just lay on the floor, unable to move or speak.

How could she really be gone?

The rats scratched inside the walls, but I didn't care. I just lay there hugging my knees, murmuring the song the Rojaks sang when they heard about Yosl. I didn't know the words, but I remembered the tune because they sang that song every night for over a month, rocking and swaying and trying to comfort themselves. Now I sang the song over and over again, not caring if people heard me or not. If Mama was dead, there wasn't much point in being alive anyway.

Somehow I must have fallen asleep, because suddenly the sun was streaming in the window. I got up, brushed the dust from the maid's uniform that I had never taken off the previous night, and walked to the gate with my papers as if nothing had happened. Beyond the gate I looked out at the long marsh grasses and the row of scraggly trees that marked the beginning of the forest. Everything was newly green. It should have given me hope, but it didn't. Tonight I would escape, or be shot trying. Either way, it didn't seem to matter.

If the commander's wife knew or suspected anything, she didn't show it. I wished I could have asked her. Maybe she knew what had happened to Mama. Georg said not everyone was killed. Some people were sent away. They still needed people to work and Mama was strong. *Mama is not dead!* I thought the words over and over again as I rubbed at a berry stain that straddled both sides of a crack in the sink. Mama was a survivor. I had to remember that. I had to remember the way she always stood—straight and tall, fearless. I imagined Mama getting into a train, twisting her dark, curly hair into a bun to keep it out of her face, adjusting her skirts, patting an area clean, sitting down as if she were a queen on a throne. When we were first forced to move into the ghetto, Mama had opened the door to our room and immediately planned where to put our things, as if we were moving into the Versailles Palace. When the Rojaks arrived later that afternoon, Mama welcomed them with tea served on the china she'd saved several weeks' wages to buy in Berlin. It was always important for Mama to have nice things. Better to have a few nice things than a lot of *drek*, she always said.

I rubbed the stain so hard that bits of polish came off with the juice, leaving a dirty patch of rust. The patch kept getting bigger, but I kept rubbing, my arms shaking. How would I escape? The guards were everywhere. I'd probably be shot. I scrubbed harder, trying to stop worrying so much, but I couldn't help it. Even if I made it to the forest, what would I do when I got there? Where would I sleep? I didn't have a tent or any warm clothes, just a plain cloth coat that was too small and worn with holes. I should bring the long underwear that Mama sewed for me last year. What else? I couldn't take Mama's china. I should take her cameo pin and pearl necklace—and the picture of my father, Grisha.

Why had the Nazis closed the factory? Why had they taken the people who were healthy, who were supporting the war? They'd already had a selection just last month. Everyone in the ghetto, even the members of the Jewish Police, had been ordered to line up in the main square. We stood out in the cold for hours until a Nazi commander asked us some questions and they sent us to another line. We kept standing there until everyone had been divided up into two lines. Then we watched as the soldiers marched the people on the other line out of the ghetto, and we never saw them again. I knew better than to ask Mama what happened to them. She would have just called me a worrier.

At dusk I walked home slowly. Fritz was at the gate and he smiled and touched my hand as I showed him my papers, but I didn't say anything. I walked as quickly as I could to our building and climbed the stairs to our room.

Just as I was about to put my key in the door, I heard a noise—footsteps. Someone was in the apartment. The soldiers! They were taking Mama's things! They'd find the pearls and the cameo, all Mama's treasures.

They'd find me!

I bent down and tried to look through the keyhole. The footsteps stopped. The apartment was quiet again. Were they waiting for me? Where could I hide? Should I go back to the streets? It was almost curfew. When Georg came, how would he find me?

I leaned against the wall behind the door, hoping the soldiers wouldn't see me when they left. Then I waited.

No one came out. They must be waiting for me. Or waiting for Georg. That was it. They knew about the plan and they were waiting here to arrest Georg! I needed to leave so I wouldn't put him in danger! No, that would put him in more danger. He'd enter the apartment looking for me and find the soldiers. The best thing to do would be to tiptoe down to the landing and warn him when he set foot in the building. I started quietly down the stairs.

"Halina!"

The door opened, and a familiar face appeared in the crack of dim light.

"Batya?"

"Shh." She grabbed my arm and led me inside, then closed the door.

"Wasn't everyone at the factory taken? I thought you were the soldiers."

"I heard you humming and waited for you to come in. When you didn't, I got worried."

"I was humming! I'm so stupid. What if you were . . ."

"It doesn't matter," Batya said. "You must gather your things. Georg came a little while ago. He is coming back soon."

"What happened? Did Mama escape, too?"

"I don't think so. I hid when they were taking everyone to the fort and—" Batya covered her face with her hands. Her long black braid curved over her shoulders.

"Did you see?"

"They took my father and brothers; they took all the men away and put them on a train. There was a deep pit. They told the women—"

"No!"

"Shh!" I felt Batya's arms around me as she reached up and pressed her hand over my mouth. "You can't let anyone hear us. It will endanger the whole—"

"Did you see Mama?"

"I ran when I heard the gunshots. A messenger found me. He said it would be safer to return to the ghetto and escape with the others tonight, so he put me in a sack of potatoes and brought me back through the gate. Go and get ready. Wear as much as you can."

"But did you see Mama?"

"She was in the line with the other women." Batya spoke softly, squeezing me tighter. "But you can't think about that now. She'd want you to save yourself."

Batya unwrapped her arms and tried to break away from me, but I held on to her, burying my face in her thick braid, which smelled like potatoes. It was just yesterday that I'd held on to Mama like that, before I'd left for the commander's house and she'd left for the factory. If only we had known what would happen. I would have just held on and on. I would have tried to remember everything she said to me. I would have insisted that we hold hands before we got to the ghetto gate, the way we used to when we walked together in Berlin. I would have sung one last song for her.

"We must get ready," Batya said again, breaking away more firmly. "Take some of your mother's things so you can remember her."

I opened the wardrobe. There wasn't much left. The Nazis had taken most of our possessions. On the top shelf were three tubes of red lipstick worn down to the bottom and a compact. Hanging below was a heavy black coat, a red umbrella, and two dresses—one pine green and one navy blue. In the pocket of the green dress were Mama's pearls and cameo pin, along with an embroidered linen handkerchief. I put these in Mama's coat pocket and put on the coat, feeling the weight of Mama's body and that perfumy, smoky smell.

The coat felt heavy, so heavy, I suddenly couldn't move. I sank to the floor and let the tears roll down my face, biting my lip to keep myself from making noise.

"Halina, get up right now! We don't have much time!" Batya scurried around gathering long underwear, wool stockings, and sweaters. "Put these on."

I let Batya slide my legs into the underwear and stockings, and put the picture of my father into Mama's coat pocket. Batya gave me two potatoes. She rolled up Mama's two dresses and stuffed them into the sleeve of the coat; she put an extra pair of stockings in a sweater pocket, and grabbed Mama's fur hat, which had been stuffed into a crack in the floorboard. Mama had hidden the hat when the Nazis ordered us to give up our furs.

"Hide this hat somewhere," Batya said as she put her father's *tallis* and *tefillin* into the pocket of her older brother's large coat. "We should *daven Ma'ariv*. My father would want us to, even if we're girls."

What good would that do? I wanted to say, but I merely nodded and listened politely as Batya murmured the Rojak family's familiar evening chants under her breath.

"Now *Kaddish* . . . ," Batya said. "For your mother."

We stood together as Batya murmured the prayer for the dead. Only then did her voice break. "I'm doing it all wrong! When my mother died, we lit *Yahrzeit* candles. We didn't leave the house for seven days."

"That was before the war. You didn't do that when Yosl disappeared."

"We didn't know that he was truly dead."

"But maybe . . ."

"I saw her at the edge of the pit. I heard . . ."

I covered my ears. "I have a candle."

"We can't light it. Someone might see!"

"We'll just light it for a minute—away from the window. Then we'll blow it out."

As Batya lit the candle, I imagined that Mama's spirit was in the flame, which rose high in the darkness, a large orange triangle whose tip pointed to the sky. We sat holding hands in the dark, watching the flame shift its shape with the passing currents. That was how I'd have to be now, I thought. Ready to move wherever I had to. Mama wouldn't want me to sink uselessly on the floor and be caught by the Nazis. Mama would want me to be brave and strong. Mama would want me to do whatever I could to survive.

There was a knock on the door. "We're ready," Georg whispered softly. "Come."

chapter
three

Georg led us through a narrow alleyway. We climbed
some stairs, then turned a corner.

"Halt!" A voice came out of the darkness. "Where are you
going?"

"These girls are going to pray at the synagogue," Georg's
voice was smooth as he confronted the German guard, but his
grip on my wrist was sweaty. "I am escorting them to make sure
that they arrive safely."

"It's after curfew."

"We secured permission from your commanding officer
to open the synagogue tonight." He reached into his pocket
and handed the man his papers. "There's a party tonight in

the alehouse, compliments of the Jewish Police. I'm surprised you're not there."

The man held the butt of his rifle against my ribs as he looked at the papers. "Go," he said, shoving me hard with the gun.

I stumbled, but Georg caught me before I fell. "That's why I needed your mother's money," he whispered after the guard had left. "We used it to buy liquor." His breath was garlicky in my ear. "Everyone should be good and drunk by now."

We continued to walk through the quiet streets. Most of the guards must have been at the alehouse, because I didn't see any more of them. When we got to the synagogue, Georg led us into the basement. A hole had been dug right in the middle of the floor, and a large, burly man was sitting by the hole, pointing to a number of maps drawn on a large drawing pad. Crowds of people were gathered around him: old men, young teenage boys, women holding babies, children fidgeting in their fathers' arms.

"We have worked for weeks digging this tunnel, hiding the dirt in small sacks under the floorboards," the man said. "It connects to the sewer line." In the dim light I could see streaks of dirt in the folds of his face, as if he had just finished digging that very moment and hadn't yet cleaned up. "The water may be ankle-deep in some places, but that should be all. It won't be pleasant, but it is the only way. The pipe ends at the outskirts of the city. Then you must separate. Go in groups of two or three. Too many in a group will attract suspicion. The younger, stronger men, especially, should go directly into the forest over here," he pointed to a place on the map. "There are many groups of Russian guerrilla soldiers who will happily take you in if you are willing to help fight the Nazis and can give them a weapon or two. We have a limited number of guns to distribute."

"Guns?" Batya whispered to me.

"The others should go west toward the small farm villages. I will assign each group to a house where they won't inform on you. You must sleep in the barn and take whatever food they give you, though they may not give you anything. Scouts will pick you up as soon as it is safe for them to do so. They'll take you to the family camps in the forest."

"Good-bye, Batya. Good-bye, Halina. Be safe." Georg reached out to hug me, but I drew away. We hadn't been close, and I'd always resented him for taking a part of Mama away from me.

"I thought you were coming with us," I said.

"I have too much work to do here."

"Didn't you say they were going to empty the ghetto? You'll be killed!"

"I must make sure that as many people escape as possible. Don't worry about me. I've always been able to live by my wits."

"But my mother would have wanted you to save yourself!"

Georg paused, brushing his hand against the side of his face. "I wanted her to escape before now. If only she had listened to me . . ." He took a breath and tried to continue speaking, but his voice broke. "More than anything, your mother would want you to be safe," he whispered. "She loved you, Halina, far more than she loved me. Go now. I must bring some others here." He turned and disappeared into the shadows.

Batya and I waited in line, watching people lower themselves into the tunnel. Dislodged dust filled the room. Batya coughed. She was sensitive to smoke. Often Mama had to blow her cigarette smoke out the window because of Batya's allergies. I looked in Mama's coat pockets and pulled out the white handkerchief, monogrammed with her initials, *RR* for Riva Rudowski. "Put this over your mouth when you go into the tunnel." I pressed the handkerchief into Batya's hand, remembering the day Mama had bought it, on the way home from my singing lesson with Frau Schneider. She had said she was tired of plain cotton handkerchiefs. She'd wanted something fancier, linen embroidered with lace.

"It's your mother's special handkerchief," Batya protested.

"It doesn't matter. You'll need it in the tunnel."

"It will be ruined."

"It's just a piece of cloth. I have other ways to remember my mother."

The line around us began to shrink as more people received

their instructions, then disappeared into a cloud of dust. When we reached the man with the maps, he frowned at us.

"You're traveling alone? How old are you?"

"I'm fifteen and she's thirteen," Batya said.

"You don't look fifteen. You don't even look as old as she is," the man said to Batya, who was short for her age, and small-framed. "It's not good, two young girls alone. The roads between the villages are full of bandits." He turned to three young men standing behind us. "I need to split you up. One of you older boys must go with these girls."

"But we're brothers!"

"*Mir zaynen ale brider*," the man answered. "We're all brothers. One of you must go with these two girls."

"We can go alone," Batya insisted. "Let them stay together."

I squeezed Batya's arm. Mama told me what bandits did to young girls. It would be good to have someone with us.

"You'll go with one of these men," the burly man said. "You need to be protected."

I looked at the three brothers. All of them were tall. The older two were broad and dark. The youngest, who looked about my age, was wiry and a bit gawky, but cute in his own way, with large round eyes and a wave of thick, light hair that kept falling into his face. It would be terrible for us to separate him from his siblings. He needed his brothers as much as we needed them.

"We'll all go together!" I said.

The man with the maps frowned at me, his dark eyebrows forming a single line along his forehead. "Don't walk too close to each other, and stay hidden. I'll give you two guns. Walk north to this village," he pointed to a spot on the map, "and rendezvous at this farmhouse here. It is the home of the Orvatski family. They will not mind taking in five people. They are well connected and have sworn to help as many as they can. You must make three right turns once you get to the sewer lines," the man said to the oldest brother as we tied ourselves together with a long rope. "Then you will come out on the correct road. Now go!"

The older boys took the two lead positions. Next they tied the rope to their younger brother, and then to me, with Batya at the end. Immediately it was dark—pitch dark. I crawled on my hands and knees, following the tug of the rope in front of me. The tunnel stank of mold and old dirt. Despite the handkerchief, Batya's cough echoed loudly in the darkness. Around me I could feel creepy, slimy things, and I heard rats. I hoped I wouldn't touch any. I kept holding on to the rope, letting myself be dragged through the twists and turns in the darkness. Farther ahead I heard a baby crying, and a child whining, "Mommy, it's dark." For once I was glad of the darkness; I didn't want to see what I was crawling through. I could smell vomit. Probably I was stepping in it, but I tried not to think about that, even after the heaves came up. I wondered what I looked like, covered with sewage sludge and vomit and who knew what else. Mama would have never let me get that dirty. Mama might not have made it, I thought. Mama might have taken one whiff of the stench of that tunnel and said, "I'd rather be shot when I'm clean."

I hope Mama died quickly. I hope the soldier who shot her was a good shot. I hope she didn't fall into that pit still alive, suffocating under the dead bodies that fell on her. There was so little air and we were crowded so close together, that it felt as if we were suffocating too; it felt as if we were all fighting for the same breath.

Finally, after what seemed like hours, I felt a small current of air and saw a slight break in the darkness. "We're out," I heard the brother in the lead whisper. And soon I stood at the outskirts of the town, just barely able to see a thin dirt road that led through the rolling hills.

"We'll travel now until sunrise," the tallest brother whispered as he unknotted the rope that bound us together, "but we won't be able to get there by daylight. We'll have to find a place to hide when the sun comes up. One of you girls should walk ahead with one of us. The rest of us will stay behind."

The night was damp and foggy, far too hot for Mama's coat, but it was easier to wear it than to drag it. I felt as if I were walking in soup. It was much too warm for a spring night. The moisture hung in the air like a thick blanket, and the dirt road felt spongy under my feet. Mosquitoes were out in droves. I tried to look for the darker outlines of puddles, though a few times the water seeped up my ankles and soaked into my shoes. At least the water was cleaner than the sludge.

I walked in the lead with the youngest brother, listening to the slight rustle of the wind, a rooster's cry in the distance, a farmer yelling at his cows.

"I like the country," I whispered.

"Shh! It's better if we don't speak."

Blasts of machine-gun fire tore holes in the quiet night. We ran until our breath gave out, then slowed to a fast trot. The gunfire became more distant, but we kept hearing small bursts.

"Stop humming!" He tapped my shoulder.

"Oh! I'm sorry."

"I think the guns are pretty far away, but we can't take chances."

Ahead of us, the sky began to lighten. One of the boys came toward us. "Max says we should find a place to stop," he said.

We left the road and headed for a thicket of trees on the other side of a marsh. Dragonflies with pale, papery wings buzzed around us as we walked. The grass came up to my knees, sometimes up to my thighs. The edges of Mama's coat were torn and caked with mud, but I could still smell her perfume on the collar.

Finally we found a grove of fir trees by a small stream. I took off my muddy stockings and long underwear and rinsed them. Batya wanted to climb to the top of an outcropping of rocks and look out, but the brothers told her to stay hidden in the thicket—hidden and quiet, because soldiers or informers could be anywhere.

"We need to sleep so we can walk tonight," Max said. "We'll take turns keeping watch. Reuven and I will guard for the first four hours. Then Abel and I. Then Abel and Reuven."

"What about us?" Batya asked.

"You can't shoot a gun."

"I can learn."

"We can handle it without girls."

"You need more than four hours of sleep apiece."

"We can handle it!" Max snapped.

"Come on, let's find a good hiding spot." I took Batya by the arm. "You're crazy," I whispered when we were out of earshot. "I don't want to learn to shoot a gun!"

We slept on a bunch of fir needles. I dreamed about the smell of the tunnel, and curled closer to Batya, whose breathing was still shallow and raspy from all the dust. The sun felt warm on our cheeks. Next thing I knew, Reuven was shaking me. "Come, it's almost nightfall."

I was hungry—starving, in fact—and remembered the two potatoes in my pocket. It was terrible to eat them raw, but there was no other choice. I handed one to Reuven, who pulled out his pocketknife and divided it into sections to share with his brothers. "Divide this one too," I said. "And Batya's."

A few pieces of raw potato wasn't much of a meal. It sat heavily in my stomach, but it was better than nothing. What would we eat tonight? I didn't know anything about gathering herbs, berries, or mushrooms, and I remembered the man with the maps saying, "You must take whatever food they give you, even if they don't give you anything."

"How old are you?" I whispered to Reuven.

"Fourteen." He bent his head and quickened his pace.

"I'm sorry. I know we're not supposed to speak."

"I'm just worried that someone will hear us. They could torture us, make us tell them about the tunnel."

I felt a catch in the pit of my stomach. I hadn't thought about that. I wished I had a suicide pill or something, because I knew if they tortured me, I'd probably break down and tell them everything.

The night was cooler and clearer than the previous one. Stars began to come out in large numbers. More stars than I'd ever seen in the city. It seemed that for every star, there was a cluster of stars behind it, a milky white haze of light that covered the sky no matter which way you looked. Where was Mama now? I remembered reading in school about an American Indian tribe that believed people were reborn as stars. Could I find her in the sky? I looked around to find the Mama Star and fixed my eyes on the brightest one.

We walked silently for many hours, stopping only to relieve ourselves in the woods by the side of the road. After several kilometers the area around us changed, becoming more farmlike. I could smell the manure and see large blank fields with vague outlines of small houses dotting the rolling hills, and some stray lights from windows interrupting the darkness.

"We must be getting close," Reuven whispered. "Max said to look for the crossroads once the road changes to farmland. The left leads to the village, and the Orvatski farm is on the right, just a half a kilometer from the main road."

We found the turn a few minutes later, a bumpy, rocky pathway washed out along the sides. We watched for a clearing in the trees, a light in the woods, but there was none.

"Did we pass it?" I whispered after twenty minutes had gone by. "We must have walked more than half a kilometer."

Reuven stopped and looked around. "I don't know. Perhaps we should wait for Max and the others."

We waited for a while, and when Batya and the brothers didn't appear, we turned and backtracked. This time we found a smaller path between a stand of evergreens, and behind it, a wet and swampy field. The others were ahead of us, standing by the remains of a barn as they surveyed a pile of charred rubble on top of a rise, a short distance away.

"This has to be it," Max said. "It looks like the German soldiers burned the farm."

"What do we do now?" Batya asked as we walked to the entrance of the barn. Already streaks of light were beginning to appear on the horizon.

"We can stay here for the day. The right side looks pretty secure, and there's enough hay to cover ourselves."

"Stay here?"

It was a stretch to call the structure a barn. More than half the wooden slats were missing, and the left side had completely collapsed into a mass of burned wood. There were huge ragged holes in the part that remained. Large black birds flew in and out, making a racket. Just one corner of the building was relatively intact, where a wooden ladder led to a hayloft. But it was a small corner and I didn't think all of us could hide there safely. And what would we eat?

"Come, the sun is rising." Max's voice was firm. "We have no time to lose."

chapter
four

The ladder up to the hayloft was rickety, and charred from the fire. I was terrified it wouldn't hold our weight. Abel went first, since he was the largest—if the ladder could hold him, it would hold the rest of us. It creaked, but it did not give. Max followed, slowly and carefully, as the ladder creaked more loudly. Then Batya scrambled up as if it were easy. Reuven and I stayed at the bottom, looking at each other.

"You first," I said.

"No, you. I'll steady the ladder."

My hands shook as I gripped the railing. One rung crumbled under my feet. Quickly I stepped up to the next, trying to tread as lightly as my old cat, Mützli. The loft was damp and sooty and very small, but the floor under us seemed solid. I held the ladder at the top and waited for Reuven.

The charred-wood smell was overpowering. Batya immediately started coughing. There was no room for privacy or any separation from the boys. We all lay down next to each other and tried to sleep.

I couldn't sleep, so I inched up and peered out through the missing slats. A few large brown cows dotted the pasture, and in the distance I saw a farmer driving a team of oxen plowing one of the fields that had not yet been planted. I watched the ground below the plow turn a dark and muddy brown. And beyond the farms, I could see the forest—a mass of tall evergreens that rimmed the edges of the field on three sides. On the fourth side the farmland continued along a road, which I assumed led to the center of the village.

Reuven stirred from where he slept with his brothers in a splay of arms and legs a few feet away. He sat up and blinked at me. "What's out there?"

"Farms." I moved away from the missing slat to let him look. "What are we going to do for food? There's nothing edible in the fields yet. They're just beginning to plant."

"Max will think of something. You should sleep."

"So should you."

"I've been trying." He paused, looking down at his swollen and blistered feet. "But I can't stop thinking about what might have happened to my parents."

"They were in the munitions factory?"

Reuven nodded.

"My mother was there too."

"What about your father?"

I hesitated. "He disappeared a while ago."

"They were all shot, weren't they?" Reuven looked at the ground, his fingers twitching. His hands looked large for his frame; his fingers were long and bony.

"The men were taken away on a train. Batya saw them. She was there, but she managed to hide and run back to the ghetto."

"Then we musn't give up hope," Reuven said. "Perhaps my parents and your mother escaped too."

Could it be possible? Could Mama have escaped and run toward the forest? But Batya had seen her at the edge of the pit. Batya had heard gunshots. I had to stop pretending.

"It's a terrible war," Reuven said. "I never could have believed such things would happen."

"Where did you come from?"

"Munich. We were deported to Poland four years ago. My mother was born in Warsaw, but she had lived in Germany all her life."

"We came from Germany too."

"I miss Munich," Reuven said. "I miss my two best friends, Peter and Frederic. I don't know what happened to them."

"Were they Jewish?"

"Frederic was half-Jewish. Peter's grandmother was Jewish, but their family had converted. They both went to church. I hope the Nazis didn't bother them."

"I never thought much about being Jewish until they started telling us all the things Jews weren't allowed to do. We never went to synagogue."

"We did sometimes," Reuven said. "My mother came from a religious family. My father was a freethinker." He smiled at me. In the sunlight I could see that his brown eyes were kind and large, like a deer's eyes.

"My mother always said she was an atheist," I told him. "She said she didn't have time for all this God nonsense."

"Do you believe in God?" Reuven asked.

"I don't know. I'd like to, but I don't know."

"I don't," Reuven said. "If there were a God, He would never have let this happen to us."

I didn't answer, though I wondered what Batya would say. Batya had lost her entire family, yet when we reached the barn, she had whispered her morning prayers under her breath. Was this just a habit, or did she still believe?

"I should try to go back to sleep," Reuven said. "We may have to walk somewhere else tonight, or find our own way to the forest."

"Find our own way? We have no idea where the camps are."

"We'll have to see what Max thinks is best. Good night." He smiled. "I mean, good morning, but good night."

I lay down again and watched the soot circling in the air. Batya coughed beside me but kept on sleeping. I tried to pretend that I wasn't hungry and wasn't worried. This was no better than the ghetto. It was worse, even. Mama wasn't here.

I heard Reuven's deep breathing a few feet away, and closed my eyes. This time the sun didn't feel comforting. It hurt my eyelids, even when I squinted. I took off Mama's coat and put it over my head. Things finally faded, but I was confused. Was Mama waking me up? I could smell her perfume. People were talking, strange voices. I finally focused and figured out where I was. The boys and Batya were whispering. I moved over to join them.

"There's a silo," Abel said.

"What, do you want to eat cow mash?" Max scowled. "We should go to town and see what food we can find."

"We can't all go," Batya said. "What if the scouts come? And it's a small town. People will know that we're strangers."

"Abel and I should go now while it's dark," Max said. "With one of the guns. Reuven should stay here with the other gun and guard you two girls."

"I don't need to be guarded!" Batya argued. "I should go with you. I'm small and I can crawl inside small places."

"She's right," Reuven said. "People are more likely to take pity on a girl, especially a pretty girl." He smiled at Batya.

"Then it's settled," Max said. "The three of us will go. You stay here, Reuven, in case the scouts come, though I think they'd be fools to come under these conditions. We may need to think of another way to get to the forest."

"They have to come! We can't stay here forever!" I said.

"We'll wait a few days," Max said. "If we can find food. In the meantime, I'll figure out another plan."

Once Max and the others were gone, there was nothing for Reuven and me to do but wait for them to come back. It was a chilly night, and wind rushed in through all the holes and cracks. I put on Mama's coat and fur hat, and stuffed my hands into her pockets, feeling the cameo and the pearls, and the picture of my father. Reuven crossed his long legs and sat beside me, the gun Max had handed him in the center of his lap.

"Look at us, we're like owls," I said. "Sleeping all day and staying up all night. We're like animals."

"I keep imagining my mother calling to me," Reuven mused. "Maybe it's her ghost. Do you believe in ghosts?"

"No, but maybe you did hear her spirit. Who knows?"

"I'd never tell my brothers. They'd laugh at me," Reuven said. "You won't tell them, will you?"

"My mother used to laugh at me too, for worrying so much all the time."

There was a silence and I wondered if I'd said the wrong thing. I didn't mean to imply that he was a worrier like I was.

"You're brave," I said. "I would have died if your brother made me guard us with a gun."

"I don't think I could shoot anyone," Reuven said, looking down at the gun as if it were a poisonous snake.

"You would if you had to."

"No, I wouldn't . . . Maybe I could close my eyes and pull the trigger, but I don't think I could look at a person and shoot him, even a German soldier."

"What about an animal?"

"Why would I want to kill an animal?"

"If one were attacking us, or something."

Reuven paused. "Maybe I'd know what to do—but I'd be afraid I might hit the wrong thing."

"Would you pray before you pulled the trigger?"

"Absolutely not." Reuven turned away toward the other side of the hayloft.

I looked out through the slat again. The farms were quieter now. Just a few pale lights shone from the distant houses. A slim moon cradled a patch of stars on one side of the sky. The other side was clouded. There was far too little light to walk by. I hoped Batya and the others were safe. As the sky darkened, I heard Reuven's rhythmic breathing in the silence. Was he asleep, trying to fall asleep, or just pretending to be asleep so he wouldn't have to talk to me?

I sat for what must have been hours until a streak of light

appeared on the horizon. In the distance I could see another team of oxen plowing a faraway field and the rubble of what must have been another burnt farmhouse. Reuven stirred as the sun made its way through the barn slats. He opened his eyes, looking alarmed. "Where are Max and Abel?"

"Maybe they couldn't get back before daylight."

"Yes. I'm sure they're safe, somewhere." He put his hand to his stomach.

Immediately I remembered my own hunger. "My mother told me that grass is edible, but we'll have to wait until dark."

"Did you sleep?" Reuven asked.

"Not really."

"I dreamed about the tunnel," he said. "Only this time we couldn't get out. There was a dragonlike thing at the other end that ate us. I couldn't see it, but I heard it roaring, and then I heard people screaming. My brothers went ahead of me and disappeared."

"They'll come back," I said. "And so will Batya." But I didn't think Reuven believed me. "They'll come back," I said a little louder, trying to convince him as well as myself.

"It doesn't really matter if we die here. It's better than getting taken away by the Nazis," Reuven said.

"Or shot in the pit."

"The pit?"

"Batya saw. They took all the women and made them line up on the edge. Then they—"

"Don't!" He turned his face away.

"You think we could sneak out after dark and get grass to eat? There's some in that field over there."

"They'll be here after dark," Reuven said. "They just couldn't make it back before sunrise. Max doesn't take risks. They're probably in the woods somewhere."

"With potatoes, right? And bread. Maybe even dried meat!" I could almost taste it as I thought about it.

"And fresh milk from those cows," Reuven added.

"And the scouts! Maybe the scouts found them!"

"Yes! Why didn't I think of that?" Reuven sounded happier now. "They'll be back tonight with the scouts. All we have to do is wait out the day!"

chapter
five

We spent the day trying to sleep, hoping that Batya and the boys had found the scouts and would arrive by nightfall. But despite how woozy I was from hunger, it was hard to doze off for more than a few minutes at a time. For one thing, I desperately had to relieve myself, but I was afraid someone might see me if I went outside in the broad daylight. As soon as dusk fell, I crept down the creaky ladder, feeling as if I was going to burst from holding it in so long, and ran to the small stand of trees a few meters away. As I made my way back, something glimmered in the dim light. I looked down and saw a gold-flecked stone nestled in a tree root. A lucky stone, just like one I'd had in Berlin. I put the stone in my pocket and went back up the ladder to the loft.

The darkness settled in and a damp chill enveloped the barn. We waited for the others by the window. There were no stars; instead, a thick mist hung in the sky, trapping the smell from the manured fields. I thought about suggesting again that we go out to get grass, but I didn't think I could eat it if it was coated with manure.

"They should come soon," Reuven said. "One hour . . . maybe two at the most. It's not quite totally dark. And they may have had to travel a long way."

And if they didn't come . . . ?

But I wouldn't dare say the words aloud. I squeezed the stone in my pocket and leaned into the damp barn wall. Hunger was making it hard to think. It had been three nights since we'd left the ghetto and all I'd eaten were a few pieces of raw potato. There was only a bit of water left too. We'd have to go to the woods and find a stream—unless the others came quickly with provisions. How long should we wait for them? One hour? Two? Three? And how long was an hour? Neither of us had watches. If we had to go for water, we'd need to be back before daylight.

"We should get water," I said. "We don't have enough to last through tomorrow."

"They'll be here any minute." Reuven's voice was firm.

My head ached and my body felt as if it would collapse into a heap of bones. Soon I was dreaming. I dreamed I was in

Berlin. The sun was shining. Mama and I were walking some-where, holding hands. Mama's hand was smooth and cool. . . .

Suddenly I heard a rustling noise. "They're here!" I tried to whisper, but my voice broke into a yell. Batya was safe! We would have food! I peered down from the loft, then froze sud-denly. The footsteps were wrong—heavier and strange, and I could smell cigarettes. Quietly I inched back to the window, looking for a place to hide in the hay. If only I hadn't been stu-pid enough to shout. I reached out in the darkness, found Reuven's hand, pushed it down into the hay, then scooped handfuls of hay up along his arms. He understood and began to burrow deeper into the loft. The two of us covered each other as the steps got louder. I felt a gasp escape, even though I'd sworn to myself that I wouldn't emit another sound. Reuven's hand on mine tightened.

"Jews?" the voice in the darkness was gruff. "From where? Lida? Norwogrodek?"

The man was speaking in Yiddish, but was that just a trick? Neither of us spoke or moved a muscle.

"Jews?" the man asked again as he ascended into the hayloft. We were trapped.

Then I remembered. "The gun!" I whispered to Reuven.

"I have a gun," Reuven said, pointing it out of the hay. "Stay away from us or I'll shoot!" His voice was stern, but his hand in mine was shaking.

The man laughed, a raucous belly laugh. "Is that a real gun?" He struck a match and lit a small stick. I could see his face in the shadow. He was a big man with gleaming dark hair and a large droopy mustache. He reminded me of a stallion.

"A very nice weapon. You must give that to us."

"No." Reuven leaned heavily against me. "No. Stay away from us or I'll shoot you."

The man laughed even harder. "A good little fighter! Come, we will take you to the partisans. But first, you must give us your weapon."

"You're from the partisans? My brothers went to search for food. They haven't come back," Reuven said.

"And my friend, Batya," I added. "She went with them."

"You must come with us." The man opened his sack and I smelled the heavenly aroma of black bread. He sliced two pieces with his pocketknife and handed them to Reuven and me. Reuven gobbled his hungrily, but I nibbled slowly, savoring each crumb.

"There's more food in the forest." The man's voice changed and he sounded almost fatherly. "You must come with us now. We found two more refugees tonight. They're waiting for us below."

"You found my brothers?"

"No. An older man and woman."

"I can't abandon my brothers!"

"They may be dead—or rescued by someone else," the man added quickly. "Come. They wouldn't want you to starve to death!"

"I can't abandon them!" Reuven's voice rose. He shrank back against the wall. "I know they'll come back for me."

The man's voice softened even more as he knelt beside Reuven. "Come. It is a terrible time, but we all must do whatever it takes to stay alive."

"Take Halina. Leave me some food—and the gun. I'll wait for them here."

"Reuven, no. You'll die here alone. We would have both been dead in another day or two. Besides, maybe other scouts found your brothers."

"Yes, scouts are covering all the safe houses," the man said. "What's left of them, anyway."

"My brothers went to the village. Did anyone go there?"

"Perhaps they were lucky," the man said. "The village right now is in the hands of the Germans, but there are several good hiding places."

I looked into the man's face. His skin was rough and leathery, but his eyes were kind. And then I thought of what Georg had said about wanting Mama to escape when she'd had the chance, and I knew that we needed to go. "We won't do your brothers any good to die here in the barn," I said.

"But if they come back?"

"We send scouts here every other night," the man promised. "If they come back here, we'll find them."

"Can you leave a note?"

The man shook his head. "It's too dangerous. Someone else might find it."

The man held a match for us as we carefully made our way down the creaky ladder. Outside the barn an older couple huddled together. The man wore a suit jacket and tie under his open overcoat and polished leather shoes. The woman, who was heavy-set, wore shoes with heels, like Mama's. They were standing with another rough man who wore army boots and carried a small canteen.

"This is Mr. and Mrs. Fiozman," said the man who led us down the ladder. "I am Grolsky, and this is Kartowicz." We told them our names, and then Mr. Grolsky lit another small branch and told us to follow it. "There should be no talking when we walk," he said. "The Germans are much closer than we'd like them to be, but we hope our little camp activities will take care of that soon." I could hear the smile in his voice, though I couldn't see his face very well in the darkness.

We started walking again, a long walk that led us deeper and deeper into the woods. I kept tripping over tree branches and ruts in the uneven ground, and wondered how the Fiozmans were managing in their city shoes. In some places I stepped into swampy mud so deep that it skirted the rim of

Mama's coat. The scouts set a quick pace, and it was hard for us to keep up. At one point I heard a sigh, then a whisper from Mrs. Fiozman. "It's too far! I can't walk so far!"

"The alternative is death!" Mr. Grolsky said in a harsh whisper. I could tell he was trying not to sound annoyed. "If you don't keep up, you put all of our lives in danger. We have to get back before daylight."

Even though I was still starving, the small piece of black bread I had eaten was making me nauseated. I willed myself to ignore the stomachache and keep going. We crossed another swamp, which came all the way up to my knees. Bugs swarmed around us. I could feel the clamminess, smell the scents of swamp and sweat and manure on my skin. It got hot, so I took off Mama's coat, but the mosquitoes were fierce. In less than five minutes, I was covered with welts.

"How much farther is it?" Mrs. Fiozman whispered.

"Another two kilometers. We would get there more quickly if you walked faster. It's almost dawn."

I tried to walk more quickly, but the Fiozmans fell farther behind. Reuven kept watching out and waiting for them, offering his hand to help guide the older couple over the rough spots, while I concentrated on making sure I knew where the scouts were.

It was daylight by the time we came to a small clearing. I saw two odd-looking tents built of branches and covered with old blankets, and a large pot hanging over a pine tree. Then people in tattered clothing began to emerge. I heard animated whispers: "Where did they come from?" "Was the escape successful?" "How many made it out of the ghetto?"

Mr. Grolsky raised his arms, motioning them to be quiet. "Halina Rudowksi," he announced our names softly, "and Reuven Weissman, from Norwogrodek. Otto and Anna Fiozman, from Lida."

The people turned to one another, talking in whispers. They looked disappointed. No one knew any of us. We were no one's friends or relatives.

A stout woman wearing a kerchief and an old Russian army jacket ladled four bowls of steaming liquid out of the pot that hung from the pine tree, and brought them to us.

"Welcome," she said. "I am Tante Rosa. You are our *mishpokha* now, our family."

"My brothers? Did anyone find my brothers?" Reuven asked.

"We will discuss it later in the commander's *ziemlanka*," Mr. Grolsky said. "Come, sit with us and have some soup."

There were close to a hundred people eating by the tents. Many were elderly, and there were a few children, too. The soup didn't look like much—a few thin slices of potatoes and beets cooked in a large amount of water. But when I tasted it, I was amazed! There must have been some beef bones in it or something. I drank quickly, not ever wanting to put it down.

"Drink slowly," Tante Rosa said. "Otherwise, it will come back up. Unfair, isn't it, after you've been starving for so long? God's little trick."

I tried to savor each sip, but I was too hungry. The soup disappeared in what seemed like seconds. I tried not to call attention to myself as I looked at the pot.

"This is all we have now," Mr. Grolsky said. "After dark we'll have our big meal."

"After dark will you send someone to find my brothers?" Reuven asked, careful to whisper this time. "Before something terrible happens to them."

"They were traveling with my friend Batya," I added. "She's fifteen years old, but she's much smaller than I am, with long black hair."

"We'll talk to Mr. Moskin, our commander. He is resting now, and you must be tired too. You may sleep in the guest tents until we assign you to a *ziemlanka*. We separate the men from the women . . . unless, of course"—Tante Rosa looked at us for a minute—"you want to be together. There is a small couples' tent, though you must share it with others."

"Oh, of course not," Reuven said quickly. I felt the heat rush to my face.

"Come, then. Remember, we must be as quiet as possible."

Tante Rosa told us to wait and led the Fiozmans to the

couples' tent, which I could see at the bottom of a steep hill. Mrs. Fiozman leaned heavily on her husband, but still stumbled on the uneven terrain. Then Tante Rosa came back for us. "You'll have to sleep in whatever you have. We're short on blankets right now," she apologized. "Perhaps our next raid will be more successful."

"You'll remember to talk to the commander?" Reuven asked in one more urgent whisper.

"Of course."

Tante Rosa then led me into the women's tent. Two women with thin graying hair were snoring. So much for being quiet. I wondered if I'd sleep at all.

But somehow I did sleep, deeply. Snuggled inside Mama's coat, I was barely aware of Tante Rosa's soft whisper, then her more definitive shake, telling me that it was time to see the commander.

chapter
six

It was almost dusk, and foggy. The air in the woods had a scent to it, a sweet, piney smell. As I looked up at the tall trees around me, I felt a sense of peace, despite all that had happened. The forest seemed large and endless, and the mist that surrounded us made me feel safe, especially when Tante Rosa took my arm and led Reuven and me with such confidence and determination. In the ghetto we always walked tentatively, afraid that any wrong step could bring us danger.

The path in front of us was covered with pine needles and maple seedlings. To the sides, new growth was beginning to sprout—leafy shrubs whose names I didn't know. I could hear sounds, too, a low rumble, which Tante Rosa told me were spring peepers.

"Birds?" I asked, amazed that a bird would make such a low sound.

"No. Frogs!" She laughed softly.

Reuven had been quiet for the entire time, following meekly on Rosa's other side. He didn't seem as entranced with the forest as I was. He looked bleary, thin, and bedraggled, his light, curly hair sticking out in all directions, his clothes hanging off him. I could see clumps of mud all over his jacket, and then looked down at Mama's coat in horror. Mud as thick and wide as tank tracks streaked the black cloth from top to bottom. How could I have done this? Mama would never forgive me!

But then I remembered. Mama was dead.

The tears came again, as silent as the misty rain. I wiped them away with my hand, which was also streaked with dirt, almost as badly as the coat.

"How can we wash?" I asked Tante Rosa.

"Shh . . . All in good time. Moskin is waiting."

Ahead of us a spiderweb stretched across two trees. I stopped to look at how the threads glistened in the light, and how the pattern was so intricate and perfectly symmetric.

"Come, we need to move quickly," Tante Rosa said. "Moskin is a busy man."

"Tante Rosa, wait!"

She turned and looked at me.

"Please don't go through the spiderweb," I said. "Walk around it."

We walked for a while longer, then suddenly stopped in front of what looked like a huge pile of leaves. It took me a while to see that this covered a roof made of tree branches, and there was a small passageway, leading down under the ground. We lowered ourselves one at a time until I could see a crude door made of sliced logs. Tante Rosa pressed herself against it and I followed her into another dark tunnel. At first I couldn't see anything, other than a thin line of mist seeping in from a crack several feet away. Then we saw a small torch and followed the light to the center of the structure, where two men sat on a bunk carved out of the wall. Several shelves upholstered with straw and flour sacks lined the sides of the walls, enough beds for around twenty people. As we got closer to the torch, I could see that the walls were lined with logs wired together. The dirt smelled swampy and dark. I felt a tickle on my arm, and flinched.

"Aah . . ." I screamed, brushing off something that was crawling on me.

"You're safe. Welcome to our home." The voice of the man who spoke was kind.

I was too embarrassed to say it was the bug I was afraid of. But Reuven spoke before I needed to answer. "My brothers!" he said. "You must find them."

"Where did they go?" the man asked. He lit a sliver of branch, and the faces that had previously been in shadow became clearer. One was the droopy stallion man who had rescued us, Mr. Grolsky. The other man, who I assumed was Mr. Moskin, looked very much like him, rough with a large mustache and matted hair, but significantly taller. From his seat on the small bunk, his knees came close to the top of his chest.

"They left in search of food when we were in the barn, and they didn't come back."

"Do you know in which direction—toward the town?"

"I imagine."

Mr. Grolsky frowned. "The town was taken by the Nazis several days ago. It's heavily guarded, since they've decided to use it as a base to wipe us out."

"You must try to find my brothers! They're all I have left!"

Mr. Moskin raised an arm and stroked his chin. "We can send scouts to the periphery," he said. "But we can't afford the risk of going to town. The odds against us are too great."

"You can't let them die!" Reuven cried out. "There must be a way to rescue them!"

"If they were smart—or lucky," Mr. Moskin added quickly, "they would have discovered that the town had been taken before they arrived. They could be in a barn somewhere, or with one of the few sympathetic farmers left who is willing to risk his life. Our scouts sweep the area every other night, looking for runaways. To try to look for them in the town would be impossible. Now, tell us of your escape. Do you have any valuables? We need everything you have to trade for weapons."

I reached into Mama's coat pocket. The cameo, pearls, and fur hat were covered with mud. I drew them to my nose, trying to catch the scent of Mama's perfume one more time before handing them to the commander.

"These were my mother's."

"Very beautiful!" Mr. Grolsky held up the pearls. "Some Russian soldier will want these for his sweetheart. It is kind of you to offer these so willingly. Do you have anything else?"

I thought about Mama's handkerchief, but Batya still had it in her pocket. All I had left was the picture of my father and my new lucky stone. Hardly useful to anyone but me.

"How did you get your weapon?" Mr. Grolsky asked Reuven.

"Before we went through the tunnel, one of the men gave us two guns, but my brothers have the other one."

"More escapes from the tunnel in Norwogrodek! Georg Goldmann has been successful again!" Mr. Moskin smiled. "We were told to expect a number of newcomers, but you are the first people we found this week. The Germans must have suspected. Perhaps they blockaded the main road. How did you come?"

"We were told to go to the Orvatski farm, but it had been burned when we got there."

The commander lowered his head. "Orvatski was a good man. My father and his father grew up together. When we were forced to leave our homestead, Orvatski refused to take it." He stroked his chin again and looked thoughtful, almost sad.

"We did hear gunshots as we walked," Reuven said.

"The Germans, no doubt. Probably shooting at those on the main road. We lost three men last night." The commander gazed at Reuven thoughtfully. "I pray that God delivers your brothers safely, and your friend Batya, too. We'll have to leave it in His hands."

"How can you even talk of praying after all that has happened?" Reuven choked as he spoke, trying to block the sobs. "How can you trust God to do anything!"

Mr. Moskin reached out and touched Reuven's shoulder. "I'm not a religious man," he said. "But I've learned that there are times to fight, and other times where the only thing we can do is to pray. We'll send scouts to the periphery tonight. Perhaps we'll find your brothers. Now you must rest; tomorrow you will work with the rest of us. Rosa, make sure our newcomers are well nourished." He smiled at them. "We found a stray cow yesterday, so you will share in our good fortune. We're not often so lucky, *Baruch HaShem.*"

Reuven bristled. I reached out and touched his shoulder to

calm him. He turned and looked at me strangely. Quickly I shifted my focus to the dirt floor. I knew I shouldn't have been so forward, even though all I'd meant to do was express sympathy. I hoped he wouldn't think that I liked him in that kind of way.

"You asked about washing," Tante Rosa said, leading us out of the *ziemlanka*. "All we have is the river. I'll show you where it is in a little while. And we should try to take care of your clothes to keep the lice manageable."

"Lice?" I felt the hairs on my arm twitch.

Tante Rosa shrugged. "You won't be so squeamish after you've lived in the woods a bit longer. Besides, they're almost impossible to see. It's the itching that's bothersome. Tomorrow we'll have enough ashes from the cooking fires to do laundry. I'll see if I can get some things for you to borrow. Right now we need to talk to you about work assignments. How old are you, Reuven?"

"Fourteen."

"Then you're still too young to fight unless it's absolutely necessary. Do you know anything about building or mechanics? We can try to make you someone's apprentice if you have skills."

"I don't know how to do anything."

"What about you, Halina?"

I shook my head. Tante Rosa sighed. "More *malbushim*! Why do we always seem to get so many city people? Well, we'll find something for you to do. I imagine you can cook, clean, and sew."

"I cleaned for a German officer in the ghetto."

"Then perhaps we'll assign you to the cleaning group. It's not exciting work, but it has to be done. You'll have to be forthright when you check people for lice, and insist they hand over their clothes to be boiled. The next thing is to assign you to a *ziemlanka*. I'd like you both to be with me in Grolsky's unit."

"I want to be with my brothers!" Reuven said.

"If your brothers come here, we will certainly put you with them."

"And Batya, too."

"Of course. We try to keep anyone who claims another as family together. Now, I must help with the cooking. I'll show you where to go after we eat. Until then you can relax. Tomorrow we put you both to work."

Reuven wandered off wordlessly back to the tent where he had slept. I decided to explore, taking careful notes about where I was in the forest so I wouldn't get lost. I picked up several interesting rocks as I wandered past piles of branches and leaves, obviously other *ziemlankas* arranged randomly among clumps of large and skinny pines. People were beginning to emerge out of them, lots of people. I realized that there were several groups spread over the forest, with far more people than the hundred or so who had greeted us. Sometimes I couldn't even recognize the *ziemlankas,* they were so well camouflaged, until I saw someone come out from what looked like a clump of leaves on the ground.

I continued to walk through the woods until I found a large rock, where I sat down, emptied my pockets, and surveyed my treasures. None of the rocks were mica-flecked, but a few had quartz deposits. One had a gorgeous red streak; another was so smooth it felt like silk. The rock I sat on had soft green moss along the sides. I traced my fingers through it, then arranged my rocks in the moss. This big rock would be my friend, I thought. A friend I could count on not to disappear. It looked like it had been in that spot for a long, long time.

The fog began to lift and the stars came out. It was so beautiful, I could almost feel happy, if it weren't for the weight of Mama being gone. And Batya. Was she dead too? I didn't want to believe that. I had to hope that she would come back. A sliver of moon drifted into view. If God does exist, He'd have to be right here, I thought, in that starry sky. I closed my eyes and tried to remember some of the words of the Rojaks' evening prayers. But all I knew was the tune. Bring Batya back, I thought to the sky, as I hummed the chant, as best as I could remember it.

chapter
seven

O n my way back to the encampment, I picked up a
number of rocks and put them in my pocket. I would
set up my new collection by the big rock, I decided, all except
my lucky stone, which I'd carry with me.

"There you are!" Tante Rosa came clucking over to me
holding a small bowl filled with meat and bread. "Eat slowly, or
else you won't be able to keep it down."

I didn't have a utensil. Some of the men were eating with
pocketknives. The rest of the people were picking up the meat
with their fingers. I tried to manage as daintily as possible, but
the grease dripped through my fingers onto the sleeves of
Mama's coat. I hoped I'd be able to wash it soon.

Then Reuven came over, followed by the Fiozmans.

"Such a *sheyne meydele*." Mrs. Fiozman cupped my chin in her hand. "Such beautiful curly hair. It's a shame such a pretty girl like you is all alone in the woods."

I smiled at her. People didn't often call me pretty. Of course, she was probably just making conversation.

"I can't eat with my fingers!" she said. "It's uncivilized. We're like animals here!"

"But it's nice to have meat."

"My clothes are dirty," she said. "They promised us we could wash. I tried. The river is too cold."

"Anna, we should be thankful that we're still alive," Mr. Fiozman said.

"But what kind of life is this, Max?"

"I found a wonderful rock," I told Reuven. "It's quiet there, and peaceful. It makes me feel almost safe."

He didn't answer me. I saw that he'd barely touched his food.

"It won't make your brothers come any faster if you don't eat," I said.

"If they don't come, there's no point in eating," he said, handing his bowl to me.

I didn't want to eat his share, but I didn't want it to be wasted. I offered it to Mrs. Fiozman.

"I can't eat off a stranger's plate!" She waved the bowl away. "Think of the germs! We'll all die of dysentery!"

Bits of conversation filtered through to us. Some people were talking about grenading a railroad line several kilometers to the south, others about the Russian detachment that had recently raided a nearby village.

"No one likes the Jews," I heard a man's voice in the darkness. "The Russian partisans are just using us to fix their guns. They knew we were planning to get food from that village!"

"Shah! We don't have enough guns to complain about the Russians."

"They just expelled all the Jews in their unit and sent them to us, as if we don't already have enough mouths to feed. What does Moskin think he's doing? Welcoming them with open arms, as if meat grows on trees." The voice was familiar, though I couldn't place it.

There was a chuckle. "God did send us that wandering cow. Our modern-day manna."

"One cow can't feed all these people!" a familiar voice rose above the background, and I recognized it as Mr. Grolsky's. "And is God going to send a cow every day? I think not."

"Is there a problem here?"

"No, not at all."

"We can have differences of opinion, but dissension will not be tolerated. The woods are large. Perhaps you might wish to find a different place to live." I recognized Mr. Moskin's deep voice.

"No, sir," Mr. Grolsky said. He sounded the way I did when I was angry at Mama, and had to try not to show it.

"Opinions you may have," Mr. Moskin said, "but creating opposition is a punishable offense. Do I make myself understood?"

"Yes, sir."

The man's footsteps were loud as he walked away.

"I wonder what they were fighting about," I whispered to Reuven. "Don't they want us here?"

"Some of the fighters think there are too many mouths to feed," he whispered back. "I heard them talking."

"I wonder where they get all the food."

"I don't know."

"It's so dark!" Mrs. Fiozman said. "Otto, it's so dark, where do we go now?"

"They're going to assign us to a *ziemlanka*."

"Ugh! Not underground! We're living like moles, like rodents. Otto, I can't stay here!"

"Shah, Anna!"

"Let's go back to Lida. At least there we had a roof over our heads."

"And who knows how long we'd have such a roof! You saw how many people were taken out last week."

"I need to be indoors. Not outside like a wild animal!"

I wondered if Mama would have felt that way. I reached

into my pocket and took out the stones I'd collected. They felt solid and whole in my hand, and that was kind of how I felt being here, much safer than I had in the ghetto. I liked being outside and away from things, and I liked the smells of the soil and the sounds of the spring peepers. I wished Mama were with me, but I was glad that I was here.

"There you are," Tante Rosa called. She was holding up a lit pine bough, which illuminated her face. "Tomorrow I'll give all of you your own lights. It's almost impossible to find the *ziemlankas* in the dark. And we hope it's pretty hard in the daylight, too." She chuckled. "At least for the Germans. Come, you'll all be staying with us."

She took my hand; her fingers were surprisingly warm. We walked for what seemed like at least twenty minutes.

"I hadn't realized the encampment was so big," I said.

"Grolsky's unit is a bit farther away from the rest. He wanted it that way. He likes to pretend he's the leader of the whole place." She was quiet for a minute. "Yitzhak's a good man, but I worry about him. He has good ideas, but he doesn't have the personal support that Moskin has."

"I thought he'd be the one looking for my brothers tonight," Reuven said.

"No, the scouts take turns. But there are good, strong people who are searching. If it is possible to find them, we will."

A few paces behind us, Mrs. Fiozman moaned.

"It's unfair that these people are here and my brothers are not!" Reuven whispered to me, a little too loudly. I hoped they hadn't heard him.

"Here we are," Tante Rosa said. "Bend low."

We walked down another steep slope, then spied the dot of flame at the end of a long tunnel. As I moved closer, I could see an additional point of light balanced on a narrow, dug-out shelf. Sitting across from it were two young children. The older girl looked no more than five, and she had her arm around her sister, a sullen, curly-haired copy of herself, except that the younger girl's thumb was thrust into her mouth.

"This is Halina," Tante Rosa said. "She will be your big sister. And this is Reuven. He will be your brother. This is Mr. and Mrs. Fiozman." She turned to me. "These are my children, Shayna and D'vora. You'll share their bunk."

"I want to sleep with Mama!" The older girl burst into tears.

"Shah . . . you have a big sister now," Tante Rosa said. She turned to me again. "They will be fine when they get to know you. They're good girls, brave girls, right?"

The younger girl, Shayna, thrust her thumb into her mouth again. I went over to her. "You have beautiful hair," I said. "You look like a princess."

The girl smiled. "I am a princess. And you are the queen. Let's go to our castle." She reached out her hand. Her fingers were sweaty and greasy. She probably hadn't washed off the meat juices, and neither had I.

"Where can we wash our hands?" I asked Tante Rosa.

"It's too dark to go to the river at night. We usually wipe our hands on these rags before bedtime."

"Our castle's over here. These are our animals." Shayna led me to a bunk and put a handful of rocks in my hand.

"Do you like rocks too?" I asked.

"These are animals," Shayna said.

I looked over at Reuven to see if he wanted to help me, but he was lying on one of the beds, his face buried. The Fiozmans were sitting on the lowest empty shelf, looking afraid to lie down in the straw. I wondered if they'd sleep like that.

"Your sister might want to play," I said to the older girl, who was burrowing her face into Tante Rosa's skirt. "Do you want to play, D'vora?"

"No."

"Go play," Tante Rosa said.

"No!"

"Mama has things to do."

"Don't leave, Mama!"

Tante Rosa knelt down and I could hear the edge in her voice as she spoke. "Sometimes Mama has to leave. But you are brave girls, and you are safe here. And now you have a big sister who can take care of you when I can't. Now go and play."

"I don't want to!"

"Go play." Tante Rosa's voice was firm.

D'vora sniffled as she came over to join us. "You're the prince," Shayna said.

"I want to be the princess!"

"I'm the princess. There has to be a prince."

"I'll be the prince," I said. "You can be the queen."

This seemed to please D'vora, because she suddenly sat down on my lap, and took the rock animals out of my hand. "Here's my doggie," she said. "I used to have a doggie, and a kitty, too. They had to go to sleep when the soldiers came."

"I had a kitty too," I said. "A big white kitty named Mützli."

It wasn't hard to play with the children. Shayna took charge, telling both of us what to do. We fed the dogs and cats and put them in the stables. Then we went to sleep—first pretend, and then for real. I slept soundly, enjoying Shayna's moist breath on my arm and D'vora's silky hair on my opposite shoulder.

chapter
eight

The next thing I was aware of was Tante Rosa shaking me awake. "They found your friend!" She beamed at me as she took my hands into her own.

"They found Batya? Where is she?"

"She's in our infirmary. We're lucky to have several doctors in our encampment, and nurses, too," Tante Rosa said. "Don't worry. The doctor expects her to make a full recovery, but she must rest. She was in severe shock when they found her."

"What about my brothers?" I heard Reuven call in the darkness.

Tante Rosa lowered her voice. "No sign of them. Of course, there's no harm in being hopeful."

"We need to talk to her!" Reuven's voice was urgent. "Maybe she knows where they are."

"She may still be unconscious."

"Unconscious!"

"I told you, she was in shock."

"But I didn't realize . . ."

Tante Rosa patted my hand. "The doctor expects her to recover, but no visitors until tomorrow."

"But she might know where my brothers are! Can't the doctor ask her?"

"I'll talk to him," Tante Rosa said. "Perhaps you can try to see her after the evening meal. Right now you should get your breakfast quickly, and then you both have work to do."

She handed us each a bowl of boiled potatoes, cooked on the small stove in the *ziemlanka*, and a cup of hot liquid that I couldn't recognize.

"What is this?" I asked.

"Chicory. It's the closest we have to coffee. Now, Halina, you will help with the laundering. All the women are working on laundry today. Reuven, you can help some of the men chop wood. Yitzhak is right outside. He will show you where to go."

"What about our clothes? Can we wash them?"

Tante Rosa gazed carefully at the coat. "I'm not sure the coat will hold up, but we can try to scrub it down. If you take off your things, I will give you some extras to wear." She looked at my feet. "Your shoes are splitting at the seams. Soon you'll be wearing rags on your feet. You need good, sturdy boots. They're hard to come by, but I'll see what I can do."

I followed Reuven and Tante Rosa outside. It was a cold morning, but the sky was blue.

"It's going to be a nice day," I said.

Reuven looked at the ground. "I wish I knew what happened to my brothers."

"We'll go and see Batya as soon as they let us."

Yitzhak Grolsky came over. "I need a young, strong boy like you." He put his arm around Reuven's shoulder. "Come, I'll show you where to go."

"Remember to tell the doctor to ask Batya about my brothers," Reuven said to Tante Rosa. "Halina, I'll meet you here after our work is done. We'll see what we can find out."

Tante Rosa's girls were waiting outside for me. Shayna did not want to walk to the laundry area and begged me to carry her. I scooped her up and let her ride piggyback, which sent D'vora into a fit of crying.

"She always gets everything she wants!"

"You can have a turn when we get to that tree over there," I promised.

Carrying D'vora was harder than carrying Shayna, but I felt strong and warm with D'vora's legs pressed against my sides.

Carrying D'vora reminded me of shoveling snow on the sidewalk outside our house in Berlin and helping Mama carry large bags of groceries without struggling a bit. Mama used to say my strength was unbecoming for a girl, and something about my father's inferior peasant stock. When I put D'vora down, I took his picture out of Mama's coat pocket and looked at him again, though I couldn't see whether his arms were fat and muscular, the way mine were. Mama used to buy me loose, flowing dresses to make me look thinner. Once she bought me a special red velvet dress that came with a white rabbit muff. I wondered whatever happened to that muff.

About twenty women were at the laundry, which was a small cleared spot in the forest. Some were dragging large pots of water from the river; others were digging fire pits and lining them with beautiful, shiny stones, which I wished I could add to my rock collection. A bunch of children gathered sticks to feed the fire or played quietly. Tante Rosa handed me a spade.

"Who could have brought all these tools?" I asked.

"Some we took from the peasants; others we made in the workshops. We needed to make sure we could bury our dead." Tante Rosa's voice was matter-of-fact.

We dug together silently. D'vora and Shayna played at Tante Rosa's feet. I half-listened as they made pinecones line up on the town square and divided them, sending one line to the right and the other to the left. One line was marched off, the other thrown into the wind.

"We have to say good-bye," D'vora said. "Good-bye, Daddy. Good-bye, Yitzhak. Good-bye, Ephraim. Good-bye, Shmuel."

"Brothers?" I wondered, glancing at Tante Rosa. Her head was bent over her clothes, almost in a crouch. Her shoulders quivered slightly.

I turned back to my digging, trying not to listen as the girls continued to recite a litany of good-byes. "Good-bye, Raisele. Good-bye, Surele. Good-bye, Gitele. Good-bye, Yakov. Good-bye, Miriam. Good-bye, Eva. Good-bye, Chana. Good-bye, Sonia." They must have been saying good-bye to everyone they had known. The girls flung the pinecones one by one as far as their little arms could throw them.

Good-bye, Mama! I thought.

Suddenly the pit I was digging was the pit she had died in, the one Batya had told me about. I closed my eyes, trying to block out the thought, but I couldn't. I took the shovel and began to dig more fiercely, then flung it aside, covering my face in my hands.

Small arms encircled my neck. Shayna planted a wet and sloppy kiss on my cheek.

"Mommy says kisses make everything okay." She cupped her hands over my ears and whispered, "Sometimes Mommy cries at night, and I kiss her to make her feel better."

Then Tante Rosa came over. "You've made more progress on your pit than anyone else," she said. "I didn't know you were so strong." Since she didn't ask me why I was crying, I had to pretend that I wasn't.

"How long have you been here?" I asked, thinking about the pinecones.

"Six months. We've only had to move once since then. But they say that the Germans are making advances along the front."

"Where did you come from?"

"We don't talk about the past," Tante Rosa said quietly. "We must live for the present, for each day. At night sometimes, after the girls are asleep I lie awake and think about my husband and the time before the forest. But I can't speak of these things. When I see the sun rise in the morning, I put my hand on the trunk of a tree, and think only about what I have to do to stay alive for one more day. Help me move this log." She gestured to the trunk of a long pine that had recently become detached from its roots. "It's probably too green, but it may burn."

Together we rolled the log to the stack of firewood and then started digging again. This time I tried to block out my thoughts of Mama by focusing on the rhythm of the shovel. And a song came into my head; I could only remember the first couple of lines. It was a Yiddish song about a couple's first dance together.

"Who's the lady with the beautiful voice?"

I clapped my hand over my mouth. I hadn't realized I'd been singing out loud.

A tall young man with a red beard emerged from a clump of trees and came over to me, his hand extended. He looked to be in his early twenties, though when he smiled he seemed much younger, perhaps only eighteen.

"I am Eli Koussivitsky. Your name?" He looked at me with the most intense blue eyes I'd ever seen. They centered directly on me, as if there were nothing else around.

"Halina Rudowski."

"Welcome, Halina." He held out his hand. "You have a beautiful voice."

"I used to take singing lessons before the war."

"You don't need lessons. I wish you could teach me how to sing like that. I sing like a frog, but I let this do my singing for me." He pulled a violin case out of his rucksack and opened it. Then he patted the smooth wood of the violin, tucked the instrument under his chin, and began to play the same song I'd been singing.

"What is that song? I don't remember."

"'The Russian Waltz.' To remind us that if all goes well, we will be in Russia soon, instead of Germany."

"Halina!" Tante Rosa's voice was sharp. "You are needed here!" She glared at the man. "Eli, I've told you before, it's too dangerous to play the violin, except in the *ziemlanka*. If you are done with guard duty, go to sleep so you can be well rested for your next work shift."

Again I felt Eli's eyes fix on me. No one had ever looked at me so long and so hard. I tried to return his gaze, but Tante Rosa called again. "We need to put up the clotheslines," she said.

Eli placed a finger under my chin. "Thank you for your beautiful singing." He drew my hand to his lips and strode off.

I watched as he walked away. There was a lightness in his step that reminded me of Shayna's breath on my cheek. As I tied ropes to the trees, I thought about his violin and the way he looked at me. I kept humming "The Russian Waltz," wishing I remembered more of the words.

Reuven was waiting for me when I returned to the *ziemlanka*, looking exhausted. Yet we wasted no time in going to the infirmary.

"We need to speak with Batya right away!" Reuven said to the woman who was serving as a nurse. "It's a matter of life and death!"

"She's sleeping," the nurse said.

"Then wake her up! She may know where my brothers are."

"The doctor ordered us to let her sleep. He said no visitors until tomorrow."

"The doctor is a murderer, then!" Reuven shouted.

"Shah! You'll be the murderer when the German soldiers hear you and find out where we are."

I touched his shoulder. "I'm sure the scouts have already gone out tonight," I said. "Even if we could see her, they wouldn't be able to do anything until tomorrow."

"They could send more scouts. I'd go myself if I knew where to find them. Let's speak to the doctor ourselves. Where is he?"

"He's resting. I'm only allowed to call him for emergencies."

"This is an emergency!" Reuven's face reddened, then he collapsed, sinking to his knees. "They're the only family I have. You people are no better than the Nazis!"

"Reuven, don't say that."

"They don't care about me, or Abel and Max."

"They do care about you. But they need to think first about keeping everyone safe here. That's a big responsibility."

"God is dead." Reuven said. "God is dead and so are my brothers. I spent all day praying to a dead god."

"My mother is dead too." I swallowed a lump in my throat. "Probably everyone here has lost someone—a mother, or sister, or husband. We have to think about now, not the past," I said, remembering Tante Rosa's advice.

Reuven didn't answer me. I waited with him silently. I wished I could have been like Shayna and planted a small, sloppy kiss on his cheek, but you can't do that with a boy when you're thirteen. Not unless you want him to like you. I thought about Eli for a minute. It had been such a magic moment when he kissed my hand. I was sure he was too old for me, but I couldn't help liking him. I picked at a small blade of grass under me and broke it into little pieces. "It's getting dark. We should go."

"No, let's wait," Reuven said. "Maybe the nurse will change her mind when she sees how determined we are."

We sat outside the *ziemlanka*, watching the sun set. First the sky turned pink, then orange, then a gray filmy dusk. The sky began to mist and the mist soon turned to rain. I pulled Mama's coat tighter around me. We had scrubbed it with rags dipped in wood ash and it was still damp. The mud had lightened, but I could still feel dirt when I touched the sleeves.

"We should go," I said again. "I'm worried that we won't be able to find our way back."

"No," Reuven said. "We'll wait here."

I remembered how stubborn he'd been in the barn, how hard Mr. Grolsky had to work to get him to come to the camp. He was so loyal to his brothers. I wondered if I should have waited an extra day or two in the ghetto for Mama, just in case she had escaped from the pit, the way Batya had. But Mama would have wanted me to save myself. She wouldn't have wanted me to wait.

Would Mama have waited for me?

I couldn't bear to think about that. These weren't normal times, I told myself. This wasn't like Mama waiting for me after school. I bit my lip as I thought about our past life in Germany, about the many times she wasn't there when I arrived home, and how she never answered when I asked her where she'd been. "There are some things you don't need to know," she said. But I did need to know everything, or else I worried that things were worse then they really were, that she was dead somewhere, or people were hurting her. They were already starting to arrest Jews then. But as much as my imagination ran wild, I never imagined the things I saw happen in the ghetto. I never imagined the pit.

I bit my lip hard. I had to stop thinking that Mama might have escaped. I had to think about now, not then, and not what-if. I had to be thankful that at least Batya was still alive.

Suddenly there were footsteps. The faint light of a pine bough came into view.

"What are you doing here?" a gravelly voice I didn't recognize spoke in the darkness.

"We need to see Batya, and the nurse won't let us," Reuven answered eagerly. "She knows where my brothers are."

"The little girl? Is she conscious yet?"

"The nurse said she was resting, but she wouldn't let us see her."

"Let me check on her. I'm the doctor."

"Please! You must let us talk to her, or at least ask her where to find my brothers!"

"Wait here."

He came back in a few minutes. "You may go in," he said, "but just for a moment. Be careful not to tire her too much."

Even in the dim light of the *ziemlanka*, I could see that Batya was very ill. Her skin was bluish and her black hair was matted and dull. Her eyes were half-closed and swollen; her face was covered with scratches and bruises.

"They found you! *Baruch HaShem!*" Batya clasped my hand but continued to shiver under her thin blanket. "Wait . . ." She reached into her pocket and handed something to me—my mother's handkerchief.

"What happened to you?"

"It's such a long story. We started out and . . ." Batya looked at Reuven. "Your brothers were so brave. You should always be proud of them."

"But what . . ."

"I said *Kaddish* for them."

"What . . ." Reuven's face twisted as he tried to keep his voice from breaking. Batya covered her eyes with her hand.

"Tell me! I need to know."

"We started out from the barn. At first we didn't know where we were going, and we kept wandering around in circles. Then Max suggested that we find our way back to the crossroads and ask someone in the village to give us food. We decided that we would first ask freely, and then, if people refused, we would show them the gun. I said that would be too dangerous, but Max thought the gun would protect us. So we went to the crossroads and then a little way up the road, when we saw a farmhouse with light coming from the window. Max and Abel argued about who should go into the house. Max claimed that he should go because he was the oldest and the leader. Abel said he should go because he was larger and more intimidating, and a better shot. Max said, 'Neither of us has ever shot a gun!' but Abel said he was quicker with his hands and a faster runner."

Batya stopped for a moment. Her jaw tightened.

"What happened?" Reuven asked.

"They argued and argued until it was almost dawn. Finally they asked me to choose. I chose Abel," she hesitated, "because I preferred to be with Max. Max and I hid in the bushes and watched Abel go into the house. Then we heard a gunshot. We waited for Abel to come out, but he never did. The sky got lighter. I said that we needed to go back to the woods to hide for the day. Max did not want to leave. I saw some chives growing at the edge of the field and stuffed a bunch in my skirt while there was still enough darkness to cover me. Then the sun came up and I said my morning prayers. Max was still at the edge of the field, crouched behind a tree, but the light was getting stronger. I told him that we had to leave. He said he was sure that Abel would come out at any minute. We waited, then the door opened. We saw German soldiers. We ran. I ran so fast, I don't know how. God gave me fast legs and soon I was in the woods again. I heard Max behind me for a while, but then I didn't hear him. I figured he must have taken a different path. I didn't know what to do, so I waited in the woods until it got dark. I ate some of the chives. I saved the rest for Max and Abel, and the two of you, in case we found one another again. When dusk came, I decided to look for Max before it got too dark to see. I walked back toward the village . . . then . . ."

"Go on." Reuven's face was tight.

"I said *Kaddish*."

"Tell me!"

"You don't want to hear it. No one should have to see such things."

"Tell me!"

"I walked toward the field, but I was careful to stay in the woods. In the distance I could see smoke and there was a charred, awful smell. I heard laughter and loud songs. A group of soldiers were sitting around a fire, drinking and carousing. They were dragging two bodies."

"Max and Abel?"

Batya nodded.

"Are you sure it couldn't have been someone else?"

"The fire was bright and I could see their faces and their

clothes. I ran back to the woods. I said *Kaddish*. Then I tried to find the barn, but I was too confused. The smell was every-where. I just wanted to get away from it. I was afraid the soldiers would come after me, so I walked and walked until I couldn't walk any more and then I decided I would lie down and sleep and wake up dead. That was it. Then I was here. I can't believe they found you, too! *Baruch HaShem!*"

"Stop saying that!" Reuven snapped.

I tried to catch Batya's eye. She wasn't helping Reuven with her God talk. But Batya merely gazed toward the ceiling, her swollen eyes half-shut. "We're in a safe place, at last," she said. "And you're both with me. *Baruch HaShem.*" She smiled and took my hand. Then her breathing deepened. She closed her eyes and slept.

"Let's go, before it's too dark to see the way back," I said, turning to Reuven.

But Reuven was no longer behind me. He was gone.

chapter
nine

I'd never been much of a runner, but I ran now. The mist
had turned to sleet, and I had to be careful not to slip as I
clambered over a boulder. A cold wind whipped through the air,
a roaring angry sound that forced me to keep brushing my hair
away from my face. I worried that my hair might blow into the
burning pine branch I was carrying for light. But I worried
more that I'd lose my way and wander in circles the way Batya
and Reuven's brothers had after they'd left the barn. Still, I had
to keep going and try as hard as I could to find Reuven, before
something awful happened.

I got to our *ziemlanka* quickly, but Reuven wasn't there.
Neither were Tante Rosa or Mr. Grolsky, or any of the adults.

Only a few children were sleeping, including Tante Rosa's girls. I heard D'vora moan.

"I'm scared," she cried.

"Where is everyone?" I asked.

"They're at a meeting. Mommy tucked us in, but I can't sleep. Will you stay with me?"

"I'll come back soon, as soon as I find Reuven."

I stepped out of the *ziemlanka* and listened carefully. Voices were coming from a small clearing just a little ways away, and I could see small dots of light. Maybe Reuven was at the meeting with the others. Maybe Tante Rosa or Mr. Grolsky had found him.

As I got closer, I heard Mr. Grolsky addressing the crowd. "We have been insulted too many times. I say we break off from the others and form our own camp now, before the Germans get any closer. We're no longer safe here. Moskin won't be able to keep making secret deals with the Russians for protection. The Russians hate the Jews, and they'll only protect us while it's expedient to do so. Meanwhile, more and more people keep coming. There's no way such a large group can feed itself. It's best we go off on our own."

I heard a chattering of voices; everyone was struggling to speak at once. But I didn't really care about what they were saying. All I cared about was finding Reuven. I strained to hear his voice among the rest, but I didn't.

Another man spoke as I caught up to them, trying to make out Reuven's tall, lanky figure in the dim array of lights. "Be cautious, Yitzhak. I think it is best that we stay together. Everything is well organized, and we've been able to get the resources we need up until now. There are only thirty in our group, and only ten are men of fighting age."

Then Tante Rosa saw me. "You went to see your friend? How is she?"

"She told us that Reuven's brothers were killed. He ran away when he found out, and I can't find him anywhere! He isn't here, is he?"

"No. Come." She took my hand.

Tante Rosa lit an extra pine branch and we walked a long way into the woods until we came to a path that circled a swamp. Sleet stung our faces, and icy mud began to seep into my shoes.

"This is the main pathway out," she said, holding the pine bough low to the ground. "Do you see any footprints that look like his?"

There were no footprints other than our own.

"This is a good sign," Tante Rosa said. "He's probably gone somewhere he can be alone. I'm sure he will return."

"But what if he's lost?"

"He's a smart boy. He'll settle somewhere and wait for daylight. It's not a great night for sleeping outdoors, but there have been many that were worse."

"But the Nazis?"

"We have guards posted in three rings around the encampment. If he strays too far, they will find him."

She took my hand and we walked back toward the camp.

"D'vora was crying in the *ziemlanka*. She was scared," I said.

"That girl is scared of her own shadow." Tante Rosa's voice was harsh.

I dropped her hand. Mama had once scolded me with those same hard words.

"Why does Mr. Grolsky want to break away from everyone?" I asked, deliberately changing the subject.

"Yitzhak's like a dog or a wolf. I love him, but he needs to learn that he can't always be the leader of the pack. We must stick together if we want to survive."

A voice moaned in the distance. "The mud! The mud! I can't believe such mud."

Tante Rosa raised her pine bough. I was startled to see Mrs. Fiozman. And with her was Reuven!

"Where are you going?" Tante Rosa asked.

"I cannot take this life," Mrs. Fiozman said. "I'm going back to Lida. My husband would not come, but this young man has agreed to take me there."

"Reuven, no!"

"It doesn't matter." Reuven shrugged. "There's nothing to live for."

"It does matter!" I said. "Your brothers wouldn't want you to die."

"My brothers are dead. They don't want anything anymore."

"But we need you," Tante Rosa said.

"I'm useless here! I could barely chop one tree without help."

"You'll learn. Or they'll find something else for you to do. Come, I don't want to hear any more talk of leaving."

"But who will take me back to Lida?" Mrs. Fiozman whined. "I can't live here. I can't sleep in dirty clothes. I can't eat with my fingers. I left my brassiere there. I can't live without my brassiere!"

Tante Rosa sighed. "You have only been here a short time. Take a few more days. You'll get used to it."

"I'll never get used to it."

"Then speak to Moskin. He'll send you back the next time scouts go to Lida to smuggle more people out. We want this young boy here with us. He is like my son!" She put her thick arms around him and kissed him on both cheeks. "And we need him too. We are almost out of food stores and we are short of men to go on an expedition. I know you will be useful." Without another word she linked her arm in his and led him off, talking to him in soothing, low tones, leaving me with Mrs. Fiozman.

"Oy, such mud! Such weather! This is no place for a nice young girl like you," the woman said.

"I like the woods," I said. And I did. It hadn't bothered me a bit to spend the entire day and evening outdoors, despite the wind and the sleet. Yet I wondered how Mama would have reacted to being here. Georg had tried to get her to escape from the ghetto. If she had come here, would she, like Mrs. Fiozman, have wanted to leave?

"You must be a peasant then," Mrs. Fiozman said. "My father was a doctor, and his father was a scholar. We are from a prestigious Warsaw family."

I thought of my father as she kept talking. I was part peasant; it was the part of me that collected rocks and dug fire pits and carried children without getting tired. I pinched my arm, for the first time not feeling ashamed of its thickness.

Mrs. Fiozman kept talking, but I stopped listening. I was thinking too hard about my father, and concentrating on following the light of Tante Rosa's pine bough in the darkness.

chapter

ten

Batya recovered in a few days and moved into our *ziem-lanka*, sharing my bed along with the little girls. A couple of weeks later, Reuven left on a food expedition. Life began to settle into a routine. I spent my days helping with laundry or kitchen work. We tried to make sure everyone had three meals: potatoes and boiled chicory in the morning, and soup for lunch and dinner, flavored with herbs and mushrooms we gathered from the woods.

Sometimes Russian soldiers visited us. There was a group of people at our camp who had set up a workshop to repair guns and tools, and another group that mended, altered, and tailored clothing. The Russians would trade dried meat in exchange for tailoring or repair. They gave us extra tools, and occasionally ammunition. Several of our men had joined the Russian partisans, and together they planted explosives in railroad tracks and attacked Nazi freight trains. But while these incidents prevented the German soldiers from coming any closer, the Nazis still kept their hold on many of the villages around us.

We looked forward to the food expedition's return, but we knew it would take at least a week or longer. The Nazis still controlled the nearby villages to the north and west of us, so the men had to go nearly sixty kilometers east to find a safe place to forage.

After the cold snap the weather got warmer, turning the trees a rich green. The forest quickly became lush and overgrown. The path to the rock I loved was now covered with wild ferns, tall grass, and prickly bushes, but I kept going there in the evenings after supper, always picking up rocks on the way and adding them to my collection. I took care to choose a slightly different path each time. Any well-worn trail could give away our hiding place.

I loved sitting alone on my big rock, watching the leaves of birch trees rustle in the wind and listening to the calls of the birds. When I looked at the shapes of the leaves and the way the light reflected in the twilight, I felt voiceless, small, and awed by how beautiful it all was, but still there was an emptiness, a hollow spot inside me I couldn't fill. I think it had to do with missing Mama.

I didn't see Eli after that first day in the laundry. I'd heard he was with a sabotage unit, which often stayed out over several nights. I couldn't stop thinking about him, though. I remembered how intensely he looked at me, and the beautiful way he played "The Russian Waltz." He had the most exquisite hands, thin with long, tapered fingers. I remembered watching those fingers on the violin, how lovingly he caressed each note into a beautiful vibrato. I wished I could see him again.

My chance came without my realizing it. I arrived one night for guard duty and found him sitting at the other post.

"The lovely singer!" he exclaimed, standing up as he saw me. "Forgive me. I don't remember your name, only your voice."

"Halina." I lowered my head, trying to hide my disappointment. He obviously hadn't thought about me as much as I had thought about him.

"Yes, Halina with the voice of a bird. Sing something for me."

"Sing here? Isn't it dangerous so close to the edge of the encampment?"

"Sing softly, then. But I don't think you'd have to worry if you shouted tonight. Our grenades hit a freight car today. The Germans are quite distracted with the wreckage."

"What should I sing?"

"Sing something you love."

I closed my eyes and began the song of the Queen of the Night. I tried to sing it softly, but it was hard because the

Queen was so strong and angry. It made the aria sound odd and tentative, and when I got to the middle, I suddenly forgot what came next.

"Go on," Eli said.

"I've forgotten the rest."

"That's an impressive piece of music for such a young girl."

I bit my lip in the dark. I'd been hoping he thought I was older than thirteen.

We were silent for a while. A bird called in the distance.

"That songbird is sweet, but he's not as mellifluous as you," Eli said, his voice soft. "How old are you?"

"Fifteen," I lied. After all Batya *was* fifteen and she looked younger than I did.

"Oh." He sounded disappointed.

"How old are you?"

"Twenty-two."

Wait for me to grow up, I thought. *In just a few years our age difference won't matter. When you're thirty and I'm twenty-one, no one will care.* But we didn't have a few years. We weren't even sure how many days we had.

"I hear sadness in your singing," Eli said, moving closer to me. "But we can't be sad so much. Sadness alone can kill us. We have to be thankful for small things. After my father was taken away, I vowed that no matter what, I wouldn't let anything happen to his violin. It's a way I can keep my father alive, even if I don't play nearly as well as he did. When I do play, it's as if I hear him inside me. And when you sing—" He stopped suddenly, as if the words were too painful to continue. "Tell me about your life." He drew back, leaning against a large pine.

Usually when people asked that question, they wanted to know about which ghetto I'd been in, and they'd follow up by asking if I'd heard anything about specific friends or relatives, but when I began to give an account of Norwogrodek, Eli stopped me.

"Not that," he said. "Tell me what your life was like before the war."

How could I do it without giving away my age? I chose my words carefully, focusing on things that couldn't be traced to a specific age or year—seeing *The Magic Flute* in Berlin, my voice lessons, my desire to sing on the stage. "It all ended when we had to leave," I said. "They made us go to Poland. First we just went across the border, to the refugee camp. But Mama decided it would be best to go as far east as possible, so we traveled to her village. We were trying to figure out how to get to Lithuania or Russia, but then she met Georg and before they could arrange it, the Nazis came and sent us to the Norwogrodek ghetto."

"Who's Georg?"

"Mama's boyfriend. He was Mama's boyfriend. Mama's dead."

Eli touched my hand. We were silent together. "I'm sorry," he finally said.

"What about you?"

"My father was a musician in Warsaw, but we also decided to try to go east because we thought it would be safer to be closer to Russia. We were stopped in Lida and forced into the ghetto. My parents were deported in an *aktion*. We knew it was coming and had arranged for a place to hide, but my parents were on the streets when the Germans came. They were taken before they could get to the hiding place." He was quiet for a moment. "That night, I sneaked out of the ghetto, taking nothing but the clothes on my back and this violin. Some Polish peasants let me hide in their pigsty, and I shared the slops with the pigs. But then the Germans came and searched the place. It was sheer luck that they didn't find me. After that, the peasants said I had to leave. I spent three nights alone in the forest. Then some scouts found me and brought me here."

"And before the war?"

"My father and I fought a lot. He wanted me to be a musician, like he was. I had a good ear, but I didn't like to practice. And I preferred popular music to classical." He was quiet again. "You know, when the war started, I was happy. My father stopped caring about whether I'd be a good musician. We could talk about things that mattered to both of us, like where to hide. How stupid I was."

"We were all stupid," I said. "I was happy when the Nazis

didn't let Jews go to school anymore. But then they made us leave our home."

"I'm so lonely," he whispered. "And when I heard you singing, it took away some of the loneliness. I felt as if I had found a kindred soul."

He took my hand again, then draped a long, strong arm around my shoulder. "May I kiss you?" he asked.

In answer, I moved closer, hoping he couldn't feel how awkward and nervous I was. No boy had ever kissed me before. He wrapped his arms around me, and put his lips against mine. I felt something fluttery in my stomach, and when I closed my eyes, I saw colors.

He pulled away from me then, though I didn't want him to stop. "I wish you were older," he said, stroking my hair.

At that moment we heard the scuffle of footsteps. We stood up. "Password?" Eli called out.

"I'm leaving this place!" Mrs. Fiozman said as she and Mr. Grolsky emerged out of the trees. Then she saw me. "Come with me," she said. "The woods is no place for a young lady. I can take care of you—I never had a daughter."

"Thank you," I said. "But I'll stay."

"She's a smart girl," Mr. Grolsky said. "It's crazy to go back to the ghetto. Are you sure you won't change your mind?"

"I can't live like this," Mrs. Fiozman said. "Human beings

were made to live in houses, not under the ground. I'll take my chances with the Nazis."

"Very well, then." Mr. Grolsky said. "I'll be back in a few days," he told us, "with weapons and medicine if I'm lucky."

"You're in his unit, aren't you?" Eli asked after they had left.

"Yes." I drew closer to him, hoping he'd take my hand or kiss me again, but he didn't.

"Be careful. I think he's a dangerous man."

"What do you mean?"

"He and Moskin fight a lot. I know he's talked of breaking off. If he does, promise me you'll switch to a different unit. I don't think his group can survive on their own."

"Tante Rosa says he won't do it," I said. "Tante Rosa says he just likes to challenge people."

"Promise me," Eli said. "I don't want to see you get hurt."

But I couldn't promise. Tante Rosa, Reuven, and Batya were the closest thing I had to family.

"I don't think it's going to happen," I said. "Don't worry."

How strange, I thought, that I could tell someone else not to worry.

Eli looked at the watch that was given to those on guard duty. "One of us should take a sleeping shift," he said. "It's getting late and we're going to be here until daybreak."

"You can," I said. "I'm not tired."

All I wanted to do was to savor the last hour, remembering everything again and again. I wished I could watch Eli as he slept, but it was too dark. I tried to stay alert and be mindful of footsteps and suspicious sounds. But my head was filled with "The Russian Waltz," and the memory of that amazing kiss.

chapter
eleven

A few days later, Reuven and the other members of the expedition came back, with much less food than we all had hoped for. There was a wagon filled with dried beans and potatoes, and two butchered cows. But these would not go far in feeding three hundred of us for very long. Mr. Moskin called a community meeting to discuss what we should do.

"Some meeting," Mr. Grolsky said as our unit walked the kilometer to the main camp. "He'll sit above us on his horse and show his gun if we don't agree with him. This isn't leadership, it's dictatorship."

"Shah, Yitzhak," Tante Rosa said. "I'll give you my share of soup tonight if you promise not to say anything to make him angry."

"And not speak the truth? He's leading us toward certain death. We just don't know if it will be death by German bullets or death by starvation. Our only hope is to break away."

"Don't be so fast to judge," Tante Rosa cautioned. "Let's see what he has to say."

At that moment, Tante Rosa and Mr. Grolsky quickened their steps, so I could no longer hear what they were saying. I dropped behind with Reuven and Batya, who were talking quietly. Reuven was telling her about the expedition.

"We didn't have enough guns," he explained, "so some of us had to carry sticks in the shape of guns and hide them under our jackets. We had to leave the peasants enough provisions to live on, and there was very little extra. That's why we couldn't bring a lot back with us. The people in that village didn't have much more food than we did."

"Did you see any German soldiers?" Batya asked.

"The Germans hadn't been there. But the peasants said the Russian soldiers had come a few weeks ago demanding food. I think that's why there was so little."

"What was the village like? How did you decide where to go for food?" Batya seemed to be clamoring for every detail.

"It was just a farming village, very small with big fields and a few houses. There were a lot of cows. I think we could have taken more of them, but our expedition leader said the meat would spoil too quickly. He said that in the winter we could take more animals and store the meat in the snow." Reuven smiled at Batya. I hadn't remembered seeing him ever fully smile before; he looked sweet when he smiled, and animated. Going on the expedition must have made him feel important and given him something to think about besides his brothers.

A large crowd had already assembled when we got to the meeting. Reuven, Batya, and I sat down together. I looked around for Eli, but I didn't see him. I hadn't seen him since that night we shared guard duty, even though I looked for him every time there was a large gathering. I had heard Mr. Grolsky say that several men had been sent off again on sabotage missions. I hoped that was the reason I hadn't seen him, and that he would return safely soon.

Just as Mr. Grolsky had said, Mr. Moskin was sitting on his horse. He was wearing a shiny leather jacket and his rifle was slung over his shoulders. He called the meeting to order.

"First, I want to publicly thank the brave volunteers who went on our recent food raid. In spite of the widespread starvation in the entire area, they managed to bring back supplies. Second, I'd like to thank our fighting units, who are doing an excellent job of keeping the Germans at bay. But it's taken everything we have—all our weapons, all our strongest men, and still, it's not enough. The Russians are helping, but they also don't have enough men or ammunition. And the situation is dire. Even with the food from the recent expedition, we don't have enough to last more than a few weeks. And there's no telling how long we can hold off the Germans. We must be ready to move camp at a moment's notice."

There was a stirring among the crowd. I saw Mr. Fiozman turn to a woman next to him. "Maybe it's best that Anna went back to Lida," he said. "Maybe I should have gone with her."

Mr. Moskin clapped his hands to bring back order. "I cannot hear everyone's voice at once," he said. "But I do want to listen to your ideas before I decide what to do."

A number of hands shot into the air. Several people wanted to move the camp right away, before the German soldiers came into the forest. One woman said that if we moved farther east, we'd be closer to the villages that were still controlled by the Russians and it would be easier to find food. I thought that was a good idea. Another man suggested cutting down on rations. "After the ghetto, a good bowl of soup and a bit of meat is all I need in a day. We don't need three meals," he said.

The commander called on all of them, nodding his head, stroking his chin, until the only one left who wanted to speak was Mr. Grolsky.

"Our encampment is too large." Unlike the others, Mr. Grolsky stood up as he spoke, and gestured dramatically. "We should subdivide, and we shouldn't seek out anyone else until we can feed ourselves. Of course, if people find us, we should not turn them away, but we shouldn't keep sending scouts to look for runaways. If our scouting force was reassigned to fight the Germans and get food, we might be more successful in both endeavors."

Mr. Moskin looked at Mr. Grolsky, his rifle waving just slightly in the breeze. "Thank you for your opinion," he said. "Is there anyone else who wishes to speak?"

I was amazed when Batya raised her hand.

"Why don't you let women and girls help to get food?" she asked. "Then more of the men could fight the Nazis."

There was another large outburst of chattering. Mr. Moskin clapped his hands again for order. "It's too dangerous for women," he said.

"Dangerous? I ran away when the German soldiers were shooting people into a pit and smuggled myself back to the ghetto in a sack of potatoes. I spent days alone in the forest with nothing but chives to eat. I'd hardly think it could be more dangerous than that. Let me take the place of one of the men. I'm a fast runner and I'm small. I can hide easily in places where larger men cannot. Then you'll have one more man available for scouting or fighting."

Again, the people in the crowd began to talk among themselves. "Such a brave girl," some said, while others muttered, "*Meshugge*," the Yiddish word for "crazy."

The commander clapped his hands again. "Your idea has some merit," he said. "Perhaps there would be fewer complaints about our size if we didn't restrict the expeditions to men. But you, my dear child, are far too young to go."

"I'm fifteen. According to religious law, if I were a man, I'd have full adult privileges. Besides, most of the older women have children," she continued. "It's better for us young people to go. We're strong and healthy, and most of us are orphans. We don't have families who will miss us."

Mr. Moskin smiled at Batya. "You are to be commended for your bravery, but this is not a job for a young woman. We are planning an expedition to a village north of here. The east has already been extensively raided by the Russians and there's little extra food left. The farms to the north are farther, almost eighty kilometers. We need twelve volunteers who are strong enough to walk such a distance. The Germans are just slightly to the west of there, so it will be dangerous."

There was a flurry of hands then; they were all the hands of young men, mostly thirteen- and fourteen-year-old boys who were still considered too young for scouting or heavy fighting. Ten people, including Reuven, were quickly assigned. Then there was silence.

"Who else?" Mr. Moskin asked.

"Let me go!" Batya stood up, as if trying to show off her full height, which wasn't much. She brushed her long hair away from her face and twisted it into a knot behind her head. "I'll dress as a boy if you want me to."

"We can't have one young woman traveling alone with all these men. It would be indecent."

Batya cast me a look. I tried to ignore her, but she kept her gaze fixed on me until I had to return it.

There really weren't many other girls or women who were suitable choices. Most were either old or had children. I wasn't a fast runner, I thought. But I knew I could walk eighty kilometers, and I knew I was strong for my age—strong like my father, whoever he was. But could I shoot a gun if I had to? Could I be as brave as my friends?

Batya must have seen me hesitate, because she reached over and squeezed my hand. I stood up. I was a full head taller than Batya, but I didn't stand as straight or as confidently as she did. The heat rose to my face and my heart pounded. Still, I felt proud as the two of us stood there, the others looking on, breaking out with more cries of *"Meshugge!"*

Mr. Moskin shook his head. "We've never sent women on an expedition before, and certainly not young girls. Our mission is to save Jews, not put them in danger."

"Reuven told me all about the last expedition," Batya said. "It should be no more dangerous than anything else we've been through."

"Everything is dangerous," Mr. Moskin said. "Sometimes we are lucky. Sometimes we are not."

"I am lucky," Batya said. Her earnest hazel-flecked eyes

fixed on the commander. "Against all odds, I escaped. Twice. First from the shootings at the pit, then from the German soldiers in the woods. I know I can help. I have faith that *HaShem* will deliver us safely."

There was a fervency in her tone as she invoked the name that only religious Jews use for God. Everyone was quiet, so quiet I worried that they could hear my knees pounding together. I reached into my pocket and squeezed my lucky stone, but it didn't feel very powerful. For one thing, I didn't know if I'd be luckier if Mr. Moskin agreed to let us go, or if he didn't.

Mr. Moskin got down off his horse and called the leaders of each of the units together. I watched Mr. Grolsky swagger toward him and wondered what he'd say. They huddled for just a brief moment, then Mr. Moskin walked toward us. Close up in the sunlight, he seemed even taller. Looking up, I could see a few streaks of gray in his sideburns, and the beginnings of wrinkles in his face.

"Let's hope things improve and we will never have to send girls or women again," he said quietly. "But we accept your offer. You will leave the day after tomorrow."

chapter
twelve

We spent the next day getting ready to go. Tante Rosa found me a pair of sturdy boots, which someone in the camp had received from a Russian partisan in exchange for making a secret pocket in the lining of his jacket. I wanted to bring Mama's coat, but Tante Rosa convinced me not to. "That's a winter coat," she said. "It's almost midsummer."

"But the nights can still be cold."

"And the days can be boiling. You won't want to carry such a heavy thing. Take two of my sweaters instead."

I took the sweaters, Mama's handkerchief, the picture of my father, and my lucky stone. Batya and I also packed an extra set of warm, dry clothes into our rucksacks, along with Tante Rosa's cooked potatoes, dried beans, and oats, which we hoped to supplement with berries and mushrooms we found on the way. We each carried a jug of water from the well. When that ran out, we'd have to take our luck with passing streams.

I was better packed than I'd been when I'd made the journey here, but I was still nervous. It had been *meshugge* to stand up with Batya. I hadn't really thought about what could happen; all I figured was that if Batya and Reuven were brave enough, I had to pretend I was brave enough too.

We left the next evening, twelve of us. Shmuel Liberman, a scout who'd grown up in the area and knew it well, was our leader. The night was warm, and I was glad that Tante Rosa had convinced me to leave Mama's coat behind. My rucksack was heavy, even though we weren't carrying guns. There were only six guns to spare, one for every two of us, and no one wanted to give them to girls.

We hadn't walked far when we heard a rustling in the woods. Mr. Liberman cautioned us to stop. The men raised their guns. Reuven had a gun too. I wondered how he felt about shooting things now, remembering our conversation in the barn. That was less than two months ago, but so much had changed.

"Password?" Mr. Liberman called out.

Without hesitating, a man gave the answer. I recognized the voice immediately. "Eli!" I whispered.

He heard me, though we couldn't see each other in the dark.

"What are you doing here?" he asked, holding up his pine bough until he found his way next to me.

"We're going on a food expedition, to the north."

"They're sending girls?"

"My friend, Batya, convinced them to let her and me go. They didn't have enough people."

I felt bad the minute I said this, even though I had told the truth. Why did Eli have to know that Batya was the brave one?

"You shouldn't have agreed to go." Eli touched my hand. "You don't know how dangerous it is!"

"I'm not scared—not really."

It was true. I had been scared before we left, but since we'd left the camp, I'd felt strangely detached and peaceful. Walking in the woods always did that to me. But I was thrilled that he seemed to care, and waited as the others walked ahead, not wanting to leave him.

"If the German soldiers try to bother you in any way, just start singing." Eli smiled at me in the dim light. "They love music."

"How do you know?"

"I was on patrol on the outskirts of the woods. A German soldier saw me with my violin. I told him I was a wandering musician. He took me into the village and made me play for his friends. I don't think he believed my story, but the soldiers bought me vodka. They even gave me money. Here." He handed me a coin, taking what I thought was an extra moment to press it into my hand. "There may be something you can buy in the village, but be careful. These raids keep getting more and more dangerous."

"My mother always said that worrying served no purpose." I squeezed his hand before putting the coin in my pocket. "She said that things would happen or not happen whether you worried about them or not."

"Yes, but I'm afraid that in this case, things are more likely to happen than not, even if you don't worry about them." He took my hand in both of his and turned toward me, taking a step closer. "I wish I were religious," he whispered. "Then I could pray for you, but I fear that God would only laugh at me, as He is laughing at all of us."

His breath tickled my ear, and there was a sweetness in the way he smelled.

"You don't believe in God?"

"No. I wish I did, yet it's convenient not to. If we don't believe, we can ask for something without having to worry about whether we'll receive it. Still, I may have to pretend I do believe in order to ask God to bring you back safely. The world needs your beautiful voice." He drew my hand to his lips and released it. "Good-bye and good luck."

Suddenly I felt sad and worried. What if something did happen? But I couldn't think about it. I had to run to catch up to the others while I could still see their lights.

When we reached the edge of our encampment, Mr. Liberman divided everyone into groups of four. "We must spread out as we walk, so that we're not as noticeable," he said. "But you must stay with your group. We'll stop at checkpoints along the way to make sure everyone is with us."

Batya, Reuven, and I were all assigned to the group with Mr. Liberman, and we went first. We walked single file with Mr. Liberman in the lead, then Batya, then Reuven, then me. Mr. Liberman set a quick pace, and it was difficult for any of us to keep up, even fast, little Batya. There were several difficult stream crossings, too. I worried about ruining my new boots in the rushing, mucky water, but the streams were too deep, cold, and slippery to go barefoot.

At dawn we found a thickly grown pine knoll and laid out our sleeping supplies, a large groundcloth and two tattered blankets: one for Batya and me; the other for Reuven and Mr. Liberman. We each ate a small piece of bread that Tante Rosa had packed for us—a treat from Reuven's previous expedition. One group took guard duty while the rest of us prepared to sleep. We would take turns sleeping and guarding throughout the day.

I lay on my back, hearing Batya's soft breathing and Mr. Liberman's low, gutteral snores, but the strong sun prevented me from sleeping. Reuven mumbled as he tossed and turned.

"I can't sleep either," I whispered to him.

"It will be our turn to guard soon," Reuven said. "We have to try."

"What will we do if someone comes? Do you think you'll be able to shoot a gun now?"

"More likely we'll be the ones fired at."

"Don't say that!"

"The Germans are making advances quickly. I heard people talking."

"We have to be optimistic."

"It doesn't matter." Reuven sounded depressed again.

"It does matter!" I said. "We'll starve if we're not successful!"

"You worry too much," Reuven said.

His words stung me. I turned to face Batya and squinted my eyes shut, willing myself to sleep. Tomorrow we would have to walk many more kilometers.

"I hope I don't have to shoot a gun," Reuven whispered into the silence. "But if I do, I'll close my eyes and pretend I'm firing at the soldiers who shot Max and Abel."

"You won't be much of a shot with your eyes closed."

"I'll fire first, then I'll close my eyes. You know, before the war, there was one summer that my brothers went to camp in the mountains. I was too young to go. My parents tried to console me by telling me how special it would be to be the only one at home, but I hated that week. I hated being an only child. Losing my parents was horrible, but it wasn't as bad as it could have been because of my brothers. They were always the most important . . ." His voice broke. "I don't want to live anymore. That's why all this danger doesn't matter."

"We have to live!" I said. More than anything, I wanted to see Eli again.

"We should sleep." Reuven turned his back to me.

I tried, but I still couldn't sleep. I didn't even feel tired until our guard-duty shift, when it was hard not to doze off. Mr. Liberman must have been wondering why Mr. Moskin had ever agreed to let girls come on the expedition. I had to set an example, I realized, like Batya. Poised and alert, she crouched and watched everything around her.

We slept when the third group stood guard. Then Mr. Liberman roused us at dusk and we began to walk again. I felt tired and achy from an almost sleepless day, but when I looked at Batya scampering along, I felt angry again and resolved to keep her pace, thinking of my strong father, Grisha.

At the end of the second night we camped near a stream. This time I settled quickly into a restless, dreamless sleep. We slept until it was our turn to guard in the later afternoon, then walked in the dusk toward the edge of the forest. Now we had to go even more carefully in groups of two, looking inconspicuous as we passed along the dirt road to the village. Anyone might be a potential threat: not only German soldiers, but wandering bandits or peasants who wanted the rewards promised by the Nazis for the capture of Jews.

When we reached the outskirts of the village, Mr. Liberman led everyone into a deserted barn so we could plan the mission. Three farms had been targeted, each in an outlying area. One was close to the barn at the south end of the village; the others were two kilometers farther on the western edge of the town. Each group would divide into pairs. One pair would stand guard while the other would go to the farmhouse, first asking for supplies, and then taking things by force, using the pistols as a threat.

"Isn't it wrong, taking food from innocent people?" Batya asked.

Mr. Liberman smiled. "You're right. We should never forget our morals, even in these terrible times. Most of you have been on food expeditions before, but this young woman is reminding us that we must only take the things we need. No jewelry, no luxuries of any kind. We must be sure to leave the peasants enough food and animals to subsist. If a farm has two cows, we may take only one; if they have four horses, we may take only two. We will take only as many wagons as we need.

"German soldiers have been spotted in the area." Mr.

Liberman's voice became more serious. "Though they have not yet taken over the village. We need to get in and out of here quickly. We'll go to our assigned posts in half an hour and rendezvous back here no more than two hours later to load the wagons and drive the horses. We must leave the barn as soon as the sun sets. Now go! Remember, first ask, then take. The guns are to be used only in self-defense. Come back as soon as possible, and no later than two and a half hours from now."

We emptied the contents of our rucksacks in the barn, so we had room to carry as many goods as possible. Our group was assigned to a farm on the west side of the village.

"We'll let you girls pose as refugees," Mr. Liberman said. "People are often kinder to girls. Tell them you are begging for your families who are hiding in the woods. If they ask you where, make sure to tell them you're somewhere north of the village, far off our track."

"But what if they don't give us any food?" I asked.

"You must keep asking. While you're distracting them, Reuven and I will go to the fields and the gardens. If they try to stop us, or if they refuse to give you enough food, you must draw your gun. Tell everyone to sit and be calm. Tell them that you will not take all their possessions, just enough to feed your very large family. Now, Reuven, give the girls your pistol."

Batya reached out and took the gun, stuffing it into the waistband of her skirt.

Soon afterward we spotted the house—a wooden hut with a large barn. Only a thin stream of light from a kerosene lamp shone in the window.

"Now, girls, knock at the door," Mr. Liberman whispered. "Distract them for at least half an hour, until you hear me whistle. We'll all meet back by the barn. Can you make your way there alone?"

"I know how to find it," Batya said. "Come on, Halina!"

I had no choice but to follow her as she bravely knocked on an old wooden door in desperate need of painting. There was a rustling noise, and I heard heavy footsteps. I wanted to run, but I kept holding on to Batya, who stood as calmly as if she were calling on an old school friend. "I'll ask," she said. "I'm good at sounding pitiful."

The door swung open and my heart stopped.

The man who answered wore the insignia and the familiar brown shirt of the Nazis.

chapter
thirteen

Zwei Frauleinen." The man grinned at us, flashing bright white teeth under pale and puffy cheeks. He was a heavy man, older than most of the German soldiers I'd seen, with thinning strands of white hair across his scalp. A large gun hung from his waistbelt.

"What can I do for you?" he asked.

"We're hungry! We came to beg for food for our families," Batya said.

"Aren't we all hungry?" The man's tongue moved along the lower edges of his lip. A smell of boiled cabbage permeated the room. As I glanced past him, I saw two younger soldiers eating from plates filled with cabbage and potatoes while a fat, gray-haired woman fried bacon on an old stove.

"Would you like to eat?" the man said, his manner turning courtly, his face suddenly warm and inviting.

I was about to respond, but Batya grabbed my arm. Then I realized his last remark had been in a clear but halting Yiddish to test whether we were Jews.

"I'm sorry," I said in Polish. "I don't understand."

"You don't understand?" he asked, again in Yiddish.

I looked down at my boots, trying to make my face blank and expressionless.

"You don't want to eat?" the man continued in Yiddish. Then he switched back to Polish, his speed increasing with the more familiar language. "You said you were so hungry."

I knew I had to react as if the words were gibberish. Any flicker of understanding would give us away, so I kept staring at my boots, trying to slow my beating heart, trying to remember the rest of the words to "The Russian Waltz" and the long, sad bows of Eli's violin shivering on each note. On the stove I could smell the bacon sizzling.

"Would you like me to shoot you before or after dinner?" the man asked.

I squeezed Batya's hand. She had our gun, I remembered, but there was no way to use it.

The man laughed loudly and heartily. "We can have some nice juicy bacon for your last supper," he said.

I felt Batya's hand tighten harder around mine. Batya

observed kosher rules, and pig meat was the *treyfest* of the *treyf*, the worst transgression.

"Come to the table, then," the soldier said, all kindness and smiles now. "I will keep playing your little game. I will not shoot you until I, too, have satisfied my hunger. What are your names?"

I hesitated. Should I give my true name, or make one up? The name Halina didn't sound particularly Jewish, but Batya was a Hebrew name. Katya, I thought quickly.

"My sister's name is Katya," I said. "My name is Halina."

The man raised his eyebrows. "I was expecting Ruchl and Raisele. You are very good at your little game, Chalina." He rolled his "Hs" in the Yiddish way. "Or tell me, is your real name Channah?"

"I don't understand," Batya said.

"No matter. Have some bacon, then. Since you're so hungry, I expect you'll want quite a bit. Maria!" he called to the old peasant woman. "Give our young visitors the largest, juiciest pieces."

Batya's face turned pale as Maria handed us each a cracked plate with four large pieces of bacon dripping with fat and grease. She glared at us as if we were the ones responsible for her troubles rather than the German soldiers.

Even though we hadn't been observant, Mama and I considered pig meat unclean and never ate it. I cut a small piece off the end, closing my eyes as I put the forbidden food in my mouth. I *was* hungry, and I'd eaten worse things than bacon. Sometimes I'd had to raid garbage cans for moldy potato peels when I lived in the ghetto. *It's just an animal, it's just meat,* I told myself. The bacon had a smoky flavor that was rather pleasant, though my stomach continued to churn as I watched the man watching us. I put another piece in my mouth, then looked over at Batya, who was cutting her bacon into smaller and smaller pieces.

"Eat some. It's good," the soldier whispered in Yiddish again, first in Batya's ear, then in mine. His smell, a mixture of sweat and cologne and bacon smoke, made me gag.

"*Ach!* Your God is punishing you!" the man said. "If I were as hungry as you say you are, I would eat anything. I would be thankful, not arrogant and fussy. But you Jews have always thought you were better than we are." He laughed again. "My mother worked for a Jewish banker. He treated her like dirt. It's about time we put Jews in their place—six feet under!" He laughed again.

"We're Polish," Batya said.

"Yes, and I'm Chinese," the soldier said. "But it doesn't matter. I'll let you keep telling your little story. Now, clean your plate." He licked his lips. "And then I'll ask for proper payment in return for the food."

"Can't I take this home to my family?" Batya asked.

"Where is your family?"

"Several kilometers north of here. We ran away when the soldiers came."

"*Ach!* The first true thing you've said. But I take pleasure in seeing that poor peasants are well fed. Isn't that right, Maria?" He slapped the old woman on the backside. Then he reached for Batya's shoulders. She screamed, shrinking back.

"Come now," the man said, grabbing Batya more tightly. "Let's go into the back room."

"Wait!" I shouted.

"I've already waited long enough!"

"Isn't it true that Germans love music? I can sing for you."

The man threw back his head and laughed. "What could a poor Polish peasant sing except a dirty Polish folk song?"

"I can sing the Queen of the Night's aria from *The Magic Flute*. In German."

The man raised his eyebrows. "Go on, then." His sarcasm was as thick as the smoke from the bacon. "Sing for your supper."

I closed my eyes, determined to sing until my voice gave out. If I could distract the soldiers, perhaps Batya would see a chance to escape. In any case, if I could sing for a long enough time, Reuven and Mr. Liberman might be able to take the food they needed and get away unnoticed.

I threw my head back, keeping my eyes shut, fixing on the image of the Queen drifting in on top of a large, puffy cloud, just like she had in the opera. If only I were as powerful as she was. If only I could lead this man away like the Pied Piper of Hamelin led the rats. If only I could watch him jump into the river the way a soldier like him had watched Mama jump into a pit. I sang louder, more angrily, the notes coming high and quick, and suddenly I felt strong. I squinched my eyes tighter and kept singing. When I reached the end, I quickly went back to the beginning, and sang the aria again, more slowly this time, determined to draw out my song for as long I could.

There was a rustle toward the back of the house, and then I heard Mr. Liberman's whistle. All we had to do now was find a way to escape and get back to the barn. I opened my eyes. The man regarded me coolly, unmoved, but I didn't let that shake me. I closed my eyes again and kept singing as loud as I could to block out any of the sounds Reuven and Mr. Liberman might be making. Then something clattered in the basement.

"*Was ist das?*" The man turned to the two younger soldiers. "Go downstairs. It appears we have more visitors."

The two younger soldiers got up from the table. "You can stop singing!" the older man said. "You've had your last supper and your last song. We will all go into the back room now."

His arm tightened around my wrist as he shoved the hard, cold butt of his gun against my ribs.

chapter
fourteen

The "back room" was not really a room at all, but a storage shed. From the open square holes that served as windows, I could smell the stench of a chicken coop nearby. Nuggets of chicken feed had spilled from the burlap sacks that lined the walls. The man kept the gun at my ribs as he ordered Batya and me to lie down. I could feel the chicken feed scratching my neck, and crawling insects on the stinky, moldy floor.

"Now, which of you young ladies would like to be first?" the man asked as he pointed the gun at us. "Is it better manners to start with the oldest or the youngest?"

Batya's fingers tightened in mine. Neither of us spoke. I stared at the man as he came closer, trying to keep my focus on his face, but the small bits of pork I saw between his teeth made me turn away in disgust.

"Do you find me that ugly?" The man grabbed my neck, lowering himself on top of me. He was so heavy. Even his hands were heavy as they grabbed at my throat. The room started swirling. From somewhere far distant, I heard Batya crying. I kept fighting for gasps of air, and then everything was black and still.

In the distance I noticed a peaceful, rose-colored light. As I started walking toward it, I saw my special rock, a dark silhouette in the distance. Surrounding it were all my stones, the stones from the woods and the stones from Berlin, the golden flecks of the lucky stones glimmering among them.

The light turned black again.

Air rushed into my lungs and I coughed, trying to slow down the swirling room and prevent the bacon from coming up. The man was standing up now, facing away from us in the corner of the room, talking to the other soldiers.

"Someone's stolen the food stores."

"More Jews! Go search for them!"

"The gun!" I whispered to Batya.

She looked at me wild-eyed, but shook her head.

"The gun!" I was afraid to whisper more loudly, so I mouthed the words, and made the shape of a gun with my fingers. Batya fumbled with the inside of her skirt, then shook her head again.

The man turned back to us. "Do you girls know anything about this? If you tell me, all will be forgiven. I will not hurt you."

I shook my head.

"You might want to tell me," the man said, showing his pork-flecked teeth as he smiled, "because heroes to the Reich get special favor."

"But we don't know anything," Batya said. "I swear to you."

"Does Christ teach you to lie?" the man shouted, shoving the butt of his gun against her cheek. "What does our good Lord, Jesus Christ, say about lying?"

"I don't go to church," Batya said in a very small voice. "My father was excommunicated and he forbade us to go after that."

"But surely you must remember your catechism."

Batya shook her head.

"Because you are stinking, lying Jews." The man's puffy, gooey face was beet-red now. He had turned back into a monster, shouting and striking Batya with the butt of his gun.

I screamed.

"Shut up, or you'll be next!"

Blood poured out of Batya's mouth as she sank to the floor in a faint. The man lowered himself on top of her, his hands at her throat. His head was facing away from me, so I began to inch toward the door, careful not to make a sound as the man's grunts got louder. I slithered along the floor, despite the swirling room, shuddering each time a piece of chicken feed rolled under me and made a noise. But the man kept on grunting, looking away from me. I was close now, just a few centimeters from the main room. I raised myself up, backing away carefully, keeping just enough of an eye on the man to make sure to stop if he turned his head. I couldn't see Batya at all, only a pale, white arm sticking out from under his body. But I couldn't do anything about that. I felt the door against my back, pushed it open, and ran as fast I could.

It was still light, but just barely. If I could get to the barn before everyone left, there might be a chance to save Batya. It was dangerous, but I had to take the quickest way I could, straight down the road. It was the only hope.

Lined with tall grass on either side, the road was bumpy, dusty, and gravelly. The weather had turned unusually hot and muggy, and breathing was hard, but I kept running, ignoring the sharp pain in my side, the sweat pouring down my face, my heart beating so hard that it hurt. In the distance I could see three people walking the other way: Two of them were wearing the dreaded brown shirt of the Nazis. I raced deep into the grass, where I burrowed down and lay still.

"Shoot me now!" I heard an old woman say. "I won't tell you anything."

"You'll talk, you old hag. And then we'll shoot you!" There was laughter. The figures moved on. As soon as they were out of sight, I began to run again.

The sun disappeared over the horizon and my heart sank. The expedition had surely left by now. I walked on, slowing my pace to conserve energy, slapping away at the bugs that flew into my face and bit my hands and the nape of my neck. I licked my sweat to try to relieve my thirst. Soon I began to feel dizzy. The stalks of grass began to blur into one another, until finally, my feet refused to move. I sank down. Bugs buzzed around me, but I no longer had the strength to slap them away. My eyes closed in spite of my resolve to keep them open.

I woke to a breeze that rustled the grass and cooled my sweaty body. I began to hear thunder. The dark sky crackled with lightning, and I scanned the field, looking for a place to hide. *Just stay away from trees*, I told myself. I had to stop being such a worrier. The chances of my being hit by lightning were slim, and I could collect rainwater. This thunderstorm could save my life. Carefully I removed my boots. The rain started seconds later. It dripped through my hair and soaked my clothing, but when the storm was over, I had two tall boots filled with drinking water.

I poured all the water into one of the boots, then carried them both and walked barefoot, trying to follow a stray light, a smell of cow manure, some clue that would lead me back to the

barn. But I had no idea where I was. It was pointless to mean-
der in the darkness. I decided to rest and save my strength. I
would get up at the first light and find the barn, then move into
the woods quickly, before full sun.

I found a group of trees and lay down beneath them,
propping my water-filled boot against one of the trunks. The
temperature dropped and the wind picked up; my cold clothes
clung to me, making my teeth chatter. It would be better to sit
up, I thought, so I leaned against an old maple, keeping one
hand on the water-filled boot. I drank a little of the water,
which had bugs in it and a leathery taste. Then I closed my
eyes, but I couldn't sleep. The image of the rose-colored light
kept floating back. Was this what it felt like to die? Had
Mama seen a light like that?

"If I'm going to die, let me die here, alone in the fields." I
looked up at the sky. It was a blotchy, cloudy mass. Not a single
star penetrated the black haze.

"Let me die here," I whispered again. I put my cheek against
the tree and wrapped my arms around its thick trunk. I had
never hugged a tree before. Before I escaped from the ghetto, I
had never spent a night outside. Now there was no other life I
knew.

I let myself drift into sleep then, until suddenly I felt something furry brush against my hand. I cried out and reached
around in the dark, trying to find a stone to throw, but there was

nothing. I kicked up dirt and stamped my feet. "Go away!" I didn't want to shout too loudly, but I kept my voice stern and angry.

The furry thing rustled again. And then I heard a plaintive little meow. The ribs of a very skinny cat brushed against my leg.

Mützli. I couldn't help but think of Mützli. I wiped the tears from my cheeks.

Mützli was the beloved cat I'd left in Berlin when we were ordered to leave the country. He was pure white, with one green eye and one blue. We found him on our steps, day after day. Mama didn't like cats, but I fed him in secret, and even took him into the house when she wasn't home.

"I don't have anything for you," I said as the kitty nuzzled itself under my hand, purring loudly. "But you can share my water." I tilted the boot so that a small trickle ran into the upper section of the leg. The kitty lapped the water hungrily, then meowed for more.

"Sorry, we have to ration ourselves," I said, positioning the boot upright.

The cat nuzzled my hand one more time, then slinked off into the darkness.

"Mützli!"

No answer.

Never in my life had I felt so alone.

chapter
fifteen

When I woke, the sun had already risen and was shining over the horizon. I took a sip of water out of my boot and headed quickly for the barn. We had gone west to get here, so I walked in the opposite direction of the sun, staying in the tallest grass, so I could crouch down if I heard anyone coming. Suddenly the grass shrank and I was in an open field. From far away I heard the rumble of a cart and saw a farmer cutting hay. Ahead of me, on the other side of the field, stood a thicket of trees, and beyond that, I was pretty sure, was the barn. There was nothing to do but make a run for it.

"Stop!" I thought I heard the farmer yell. But I kept running, not stopping for a second to look behind me until I reached the depths of the thicket. I hid behind a large trunk for a minute, peeking out to make sure no one was following me, and when I saw the farmer cutting hay on the opposite end of the field, I ran the last several meters toward the barn.

I pushed open the creaking door and was surprised to hear a rustle.

"Who is it? Put your hands up! I have a gun!"

I recognized Reuven's voice before I even saw him.

"Halina!" Before I could say anything more, he hugged me hard. "I wanted them to go back for you. I argued and argued, but they insisted on leaving. They said if they went back, they'd endanger the success of the whole expedition. Everyone in the camp was depending on the food they would bring. But I refused to leave. I knew you would come back."

"It was pure chance I escaped," I said. "You would have been lost and alone."

"I'm already alone. My brothers are gone. You and Batya are my last links, my only links. I still think they were wrong to go back. They left me a small amount of food and a map, and made me promise to wait no more than two days. Here."

He handed me a small bunch of lettuce and some blackberries. "They couldn't leave any meat," he said. "It would attract animals. Where is Batya?"

"There were German soldiers in the house. They took us

into the back room . . ." I covered my face, remembering the pork-flecked teeth, the smoky bacon, the blood . . .

"I have a gun," Reuven said. "We can go back for her."

"There are three soldiers there," I said. "It was a miracle that I escaped. And by now they've probably killed her! We should try to return to the camp."

Reuven pulled back and looked at me, the angles of his face sharper than usual. "They told me there was little hope that you were alive. We mustn't give up hope about Batya. Not until we know for sure. Please say you'll come with me." He squeezed my hand, and our eyes met. Then he drew his face closer to mine, and for a moment I thought he was going to kiss me, but he didn't. He turned away, then dropped something heavy on my lap. A rucksack.

"I wouldn't let them take your things," he said. "Because I knew you would come back."

I opened it, needing to see familiar objects. There were our empty jugs, Tante Rosa's extra sweaters, Mama's handkerchief. I shoved my hand toward the bottom, feeling for the picture of my father, but before I found it, I touched something else that was hard and rough.

My lucky stone.

I pulled it out and sat for a minute, the stone heavy in my hand.

"I won't be able to live with myself if we don't try," Reuven said. "I didn't go after my brothers; I told myself I couldn't go because I didn't know where they were. But you know where Batya is. We can kill those soldiers and try to save her."

"Could you really shoot someone? Batya couldn't do it. She had the gun and we had a chance. I told her to shoot, but she couldn't do it."

Reuven took the gun out of his pocket, looked at it, then handed it to me. "I don't know," he said. "Could you?"

I'd never held a gun in my hands, and when I touched the hard, dark metal, it felt strange and heavy. How could we even talk like this? Despite the number of people I'd seen shot before my eyes, I didn't think I could have killed that soldier either. It wasn't until Mama died that I understood what death really meant, how it felt to know that the person you loved more than anyone would never come back.

"Do you know how to shoot it?" Reuven asked.

"I imagine you just point and pull the trigger."

"You need to keep your eyes focused on your target. And steady your hand. Should we go now? Or wait until dark?"

"We can walk through fields," I said. "There's a farmer haying right here, but we can go when he's looking the other way. After that, the grass is tall. It's probably safer to wait until dark, but it's harder to see anything, and if we want to save Batya, we should go as soon as possible."

"Let's go, then."

He put the gun in his pocket. I put the lucky stone in mine.

"We need to come up with a plan," I said as we walked toward the thicket. "What if we wait until dusk and shoot the soldiers through the window?"

Reuven thought for a moment. "We might not be able to see well enough. We might shoot Batya by accident. First we need to see if she's even alive. If she isn't, we can head for the woods before anyone sees us."

"And if she is alive? How do we rescue her? What if we aim for the soldiers and miss, and hit her instead? I wish there were more people around to help."

"The only one we have to ask is God." Reuven spat on the ground.

"Don't do that."

"He's certainly been a lot of help so far."

I looked up at the sky, trying to feel the presence I felt when I sat on the big rock. The warm sun beat down on us.

"What if I go in and distract the soldier and get him to go to the window?" I suggested. "Then you could hide behind the window and shoot him when he comes close."

"But what about the others?" Reuven asked. "You said there were three soldiers."

"We could make noise outside. The older one could send the others to investigate. Then we could shoot them."

"If we even saw them before they saw us."

"This won't work." I looked at the sky again, feeling hopeless.

"We'll have to spy on them first and then figure out what to do," Reuven said.

We walked for a while in silence.

"Maybe Batya was able to escape."

"Maybe," Reuven said. "Batya is brave."

"Braver than I am."

"No." Reuven looked thoughtful. "We're all about as brave as we have to be. That's all."

I'm not brave, I wanted to say. But then I thought about it and realized that I was—just as brave as I had to be, not a bit more.

"You were brave to wait for me," I said.

"I had to," Reuven said.

"But you could have died trying to get back alone. Anything could have happened."

"It wouldn't have mattered. You were the one who was brave. You escaped from the house."

"But I left Batya."

"You had no choice," Reuven said.

"I wasn't really brave. I was just lucky."

"My brothers were brave too," Reuven said. "But they were unlucky. That's how I have to think of it. My brothers were braver than I probably ever will be. I may be unlucky too, but if I'm not unlucky, then I have to make myself brave enough to help others, even if I'm not brave. Do you understand what I mean?"

"Yes." I reached into my pocket and squeezed my lucky stone. I wasn't sure if I could believe in God, and I didn't really believe in the stone, either, but I could believe in luck. I had been lucky to be able to run away from the soldiers, and lucky to find Reuven in the barn. I had to go on and hope I could keep being lucky.

"Look!" I whispered. "Those are two of the soldiers from the house. They're going off somewhere. That means only the older man is there."

We raced along the road until we came to the farmhouse. "We need to look in the window," I said.

"I'll go."

"No. I'll go, Reuven. I'm smaller and they'll be less likely to see me. But give me the gun, just in case."

I crouched down below the window, then lifted my head just enough to peer above the sill. Batya was tied to a chair and covered with blood. The man was sitting across from her, still twirling his gun in one hand. He had taken her gun too, and held it in his other hand.

"Tell me," I heard him say. "For the last time, tell me where in the forest you Jewish scum are hiding!"

He turned his back to me then, and I realized I had a chance. But I couldn't hesitate. I just had to do it. I aimed the gun through the window, straight at the center of his back, then pulled the trigger. I saw blood spurting as the man fell, and guts spilled out of a bloody pit in the hole I'd made. Reuven and I ran in and untied Batya.

"Shoot him again," he urged. "Just to make sure."

I looked at the bloody body on the floor and gagged. "I can't!"

"Here, I will." Reuven grabbed the gun from me, placed it right up against the soldier's head, and fired.

I didn't stop to see what had become of the man's body. I ran as fast as I could, dragging Batya behind me.

chapter
sixteen

We headed straight for the woods. Reuven and I tried to keep a brisk pace, but Batya lagged behind. She hadn't said a thing since we'd rescued her, not even her usual, "*Baruch HaShem.*" Her skin was an eerie shade of white, almost translucent. Her eyes, which had always been so perky, looked dark and vacant. Blood continued to drip from wounds that were all over her body. I feared someone might find the spots and follow us.

"Do you think we're safe enough to rest?" I asked Reuven as we approached a small pond. "We need to wash and bandage her bruises."

All we had to use for bandages were Tante Rosa's sweaters. I pulled one from the rucksack and cut small patches out of the sleeve, then made larger strips to bind them.

"I have to rest," Batya whispered, silent tears streaming down her face.

I hugged her close, as if she were a doll, or as if I were Mama and she were me. I hugged her the way I wish I'd hugged Mama that last day we parted at the gate, holding on hard and long, saying a real good-bye . . .

"Here, Batya, lie down," Reuven said. He spread a blanket on the ground, then took a second blanket out of his rucksack to cover her. "These are all the blankets I have," he said. "The expedition took the others."

A toad emerged out of the marsh grass and hopped by my feet. I watched it disappear into the small opening in a nearby log. It reminded me of a story I'd loved as a child, where a girl kisses a frog and it turns into a handsome prince. If only a prince could come on a huge white horse and take the three of us to a fairy world where there was no war.

I made a vague attempt at washing. It was a shock to see my reflection in the pond—my hair a tangled mass of knots, my face peeling with sunburn, streaks of dirt running down both sides of my arms. I looked like a *Vilde Chaya*, so wild and disheveled that I didn't seem human. Even in the ghetto, Mama had always made sure that my hair was combed and my face was clean. I cupped my hands and splashed water onto my face. It smelled like leaves and pine needles.

"When you're done, I'd like to wash too," Reuven said. His

hair was also knotted and his face was dirty, but somehow he didn't look as bad as I did. "I'll feel better if I'm cleaner."

He moved off to dunk his head in the water. I watched the bubbles come up as he swished his hair on top of the surface.

"It's warm enough to bathe," he said. "I think I will, if you don't mind."

I turned away, making sure not to look as he took off his clothes.

"The water's nice!" he called out. "You should come in."

"Maybe later."

"I won't look, I promise. I'll close my eyes until you're in the water."

I was sick of my own dirty smell. But I worried about him seeing me naked. "I'm too cold," I said, and moved over to lie down next to Batya. Her breath was shallow, but regular. Even sick, she looked pretty, like a little angel.

I closed my eyes so I wouldn't see Reuven getting out of the pond, but I heard him shuffle into his clothes, then lie down next to us.

He smelled clean and fresh from his bath. I wondered how bad I smelled, having done nothing but wash my arms and face. But he moved closer to me as I felt the sun on my cheeks and listened to the faint breeze and the whistle of birds whose names I did not know.

"I keep thinking about the German soldier," Reuven said. "I

shouldn't have shot him. I mean, it was okay for you to shoot him the first time, because that was the only way we could get Batya, but I shouldn't have shot him again."

I shuddered, remembering the blood sputtering from the body, the vacant eyes. "I know," I said. "I mean, I know I had to shoot him, but I can't seem to let go of his face. It's everywhere."

"I'm sorry. I shouldn't have talked about it."

"It's all right."

"You did what you had to do." Reuven touched my knee. "You and Batya are my best friends."

I looked into his kind eyes. He reached out and hugged me again. There was a desperate feeling to it, a feeling that our friendship might be all we had left. I squeezed back the tears that were beginning to form.

"I never thought I could do anything like this," I said.

"You're brave."

"I'm sick of being brave," I said. "I don't feel brave. I don't even feel lucky."

"We are lucky," Reuven said. "Whatever happens, we're lucky to have gotten this far."

"What if Batya doesn't make it?" I whispered.

"We'll let her rest here until dusk. Then we'll carry her if we have to. We should all try to sleep."

"Reuven," I said, "I'm glad you didn't go to Lida with Mrs. Fiozman."

"I was thinking only of myself then," he said. He turned from me and slept.

I lay down in the sun, curling close to Batya. She smelled like sickness and blood. Then the sun disappeared; a sharp wind picked up as clouds rolled in. Rain began to fall. I sank into a dream. The German soldier was chasing us, the same one I'd shot. I saw the hole in his back dripping blood as he ran after us, waving Batya's gun.

I gasped and knocked the blanket off all of us as I sat up blinking in the rain.

"What is it?" Batya asked.

"Nothing."

"Tell me."

"Just a bad dream."

"My mother used to say that a bad dream was a visit from the *Shechinah*, that there was always a message of goodness underneath the bad story."

"What's the *Shechinah*?"

"It's like the female form of *HaShem*, the spirit form. I'm so cold," Batya said. "Do you think it will stop raining?"

"I don't know." I felt her forehead. "You have a fever."

"It doesn't matter."

"Of course it matters. Here, take my sweater." I peeled it off.

"What about you?"

"I'll be fine."

"We should share the blanket," Batya said. For a moment she sounded like her old self, determined and resolute. Then her voice changed. "I'm ruined now. It doesn't matter if I live or die."

"Nonsense! These aren't normal times. You can't expect to live by normal rules."

"No. Without rules there would be nothing left. God is giving us a challenge, to see if we can follow the rules even when it's difficult. I failed the challenge."

In the silence I could hear her teeth chattering.

"Take the sweater, Batya. You need it more than I do."

"Yes, but if you take off your coat to save a man's life and you freeze to death, have you done the right thing?"

"I won't freeze to death. And if you die, I'll never forgive myself. Remember when you first moved in with us? You felt sorry for me because I had no sisters or brothers. I'm asking you now to be my sister."

I helped her ease the sweater over her weak arms. She shivered, then covered her face and started to cry.

"Don't think about it," I said. "Try to rest, because we need to start walking as soon as it's dark."

I held her and stroked her hair, humming softly, but purposefully this time, the haunting but soothing melody of "The Russian Waltz." I stayed by her until she fell asleep, then continued to stroke her cheek in the misty rain.

chapter
seventeen

At dusk we continued on, going more slowly than we wanted to. Batya struggled with each step, and we had to stop often to rest. Reuven stayed beside her while I walked ahead with the map, scouting out the path.

"We must be almost halfway there by now!" Reuven said when we reached a marsh with a pile of logs at either end. "I remember this spot."

"I can't go any farther."

"Come, Batya," Reuven urged. "You can lean on my arm."

She blushed. "I can't touch a boy."

"Then lean on me," I said.

I didn't understand how a small girl like Batya could be so heavy. My shoulder numbed as she gave me more and more of

her weight. Then both of us stumbled as we came to a steep
crop of rocks. Reuven helped us up and took Batya's other side.

"God will understand," he said. I didn't detect even a trace
of sarcasm.

Soon it became impossible for Batya to walk, so Reuven
carried her on his back. She was barely conscious as we walked
in silence for hour after hour, as fast as we possibly could. At
sunrise we found ourselves at the edge of a brook that forked
into several smaller streams. I looked at the map, wondering if
this was the big brook that the scouts had drawn. If it was, then
we were just one more day's walk from the camp.

I slept in fits and starts, checking on Batya, who burned
with fever next to me. I gave up as soon as the sun started sinking and touched Reuven's shoulder. He gazed at me sleepily.
"What?"

"We should move on," I said. "Batya seems worse. We need
to get help."

Reuven crouched down and I helped hoist Batya onto his
back one more time.

"Lock your arms around him," I said to her.

By now we no longer had to reassure Batya that God would
understand if she were touching a man outside of her family.
God should be asking us to understand why He got us into this
mess, I thought, as we fell into the rhythm of walking for one
more night. As we got closer, things began to look more familiar,

even in the dim light of our pine branches. We found the edge of the big swamp and followed it until we came through the knot of pine trees that served as the outer guard post, where two people I didn't recognize asked for a password. It was wonderful to hear people speaking Yiddish, to feel safe again, and just in time because the sky was lightening. Reuven had carried Batya through the entire night.

A little while later, I saw my rock, streaked pink under the sunrise, and broke into a run. Suddenly we heard a loud blast. A gunshot.

"German soldiers!" Reuven ran toward me as fast as he could with Batya on his back.

"I know a place to hide!"

I'd explored the area around the rock and knew there was a bunch of old-growth trees nearby. One of the trees had a human-size hole. It was just a matter of finding the right one.

Batya moaned.

"Shh!" Reuven said. We raced onward. The sun rose higher and higher in the sky. All the trees looked alike. I couldn't remember landmarks. I'd only found the hole once.

"I wonder why there haven't been any more shots," Reuven whispered. "Maybe it wasn't the Nazis."

"What else could it be?"

"I don't know."

"We should hide until we're sure," I said.

"We have no food left."

"We can't just keep going. Not if the Nazis have really taken over the camp. They'll kill us all. Let's wait and listen. Maybe we'll be able to find out what happened."

"But what about Batya?" Reuven reminded me.

"We'll just have to hope she can make it a while longer."

I felt trunk after trunk, until I finally found the tree with the hole. Reuven, Batya, and I squeezed through. Inside, the tree smelled sweet, though it was damp and cold. I put on Tante Rosa's sweater and we wrapped Batya in the blanket. She stirred, shivering.

"It's all right," I whispered. "We're almost there."

"I'm so cold."

"I'll warm you." I pressed my body against hers, but Batya continued to shiver in jerky spasms.

"We need to keep her warm," I said to Reuven. "You get on the other side of her. Up close."

If Reuven was embarrassed, he did not show it. But I was aware of his breath meeting mine over Batya's small body, which only came up to his chest. Batya's hot sweat dripped on me.

"You should try to sleep," Reuven said. "Who knows how long we'll be here. I'll stay awake and listen."

I closed my eyes, but it was too hard to settle. Every noise sounded like someone approaching. There were still no more gunshots. I wondered if we should try to go back. Batya seemed to be getting sicker. But what if we'd come in on the tail end of an invasion? What if everyone at the camp except the guards we saw had been taken away? I forced myself to close my eyes, but then I saw the face of the Nazi soldier again, felt the trigger of the gun under my finger, heard the blast, saw skin popping off, blood pouring out, the man's blue eyes losing light and fading to dullness. A sour taste spread in my mouth, raw grass and water laced with the flavor of boot leather. How could I have ever killed anyone? Mama had said that all life was precious. Who had fired the gun that had killed her? Had he seen where the bullet hit? Watched the life flow out of her? Reacted to the sight of blood and popping skin?

Something crawled up my arm, tickling me. A centipede. I startled and brushed it away, but I didn't kill it. Before, I might have slapped at it without even thinking, but it had done nothing to hurt me, no more than Mama had done to the soldier who shot her.

I had to stop thinking about that. I leaned back and tried to sleep, tried to focus on the feel of the damp earth and the sweet smell of the tree. Things I could control.

I must have fallen asleep, because all of a sudden, Reuven shook me. "Someone's here!"

I listened and heard footsteps, then clenched Reuven's hand. Together we both curled tighter against Batya.

Another thud. Was that really a footstep, or a pinecone

falling? I moved as close to the hole as possible, taking care to hide my face.

There were more noises that were clearly footsteps. Then voices, two voices—a man's and a woman's—coming closer, but not close enough to make out the words. If it was a woman, then it couldn't be the Nazis, unless they were taking the woman to the woods. But the faint tones of the voices were peaceful, even a bit animated. Then there was quiet. I heard a familiar moaning, the sound Georg used to make in Mama's bed, the woman's voice answering in a low hum.

"Wait, I know a better place to go." The woman was speaking in Yiddish. I breathed deeply. If these were lovers taking their time in the woods, then probably the gunshot we'd heard had nothing to do with the Nazis at all. It was rude to disturb them, but it was more important to find out so we could get help for Batya.

"Hello?" I called out, not too loudly, but loudly enough so they could hear me.

"Who's there?"

The voice made my stomach turn circles.

I clenched at my wild, disheveled hair as Eli spoke again. "Who's there?"

I didn't speak.

"What's the matter?" Reuven whispered. "Answer him."

"Who's there?" Eli spoke louder. I could see him now,

standing up and tugging at the fasteners to his clothes. He looked disheveled too, but a different kind of disheveled. His face had a melted look and his blue eyes were glassy. I didn't recognize the girl he was with. She was older and prettier than I was, with clear gray eyes and lustrous dark hair that fell to her shoulders.

Reuven crawled out of the tree.

"We were on the expedition," he said. "I waited for Batya and Halina. She needs help. We need to get her to the infirmary right away."

"Halina? The little girl who sings so well! Thank God she's alive! Please, let me help you get her to the doctor."

The heat rushed to my face. He thought of me as a little girl. I crouched down in the tree, hoping he wouldn't see me.

"It's Batya who's ill," Reuven said. "We were afraid to come farther. We heard a gunshot and thought the German soldiers had taken over the camp."

"It wasn't the Germans," Eli said. "It was Grolsky."

"Mr. Grolsky shot someone?"

"No, Moskin shot him. Grolsky was trying to recruit fighters from the other units to leave the encampment. Moskin called it an insurrection. They had an argument. I don't think Moskin meant to shoot him, but things escalated. Moskin said everyone's safety was at stake. He wasn't trying to kill him, or anything. He shot him in the leg. It was just a minor injury.

Grolsky should be all right, although they'll put him in jail as soon as he gets out of the infirmary."

I listened from my hiding spot, not believing what I was hearing. How could Mr. Moskin . . . It was one thing to shoot a German soldier, but to shoot a fellow Jew!

I didn't want to go back to the camp anymore. I just wanted to stay here, inside the tree.

"No! Stop!" Batya cried out in her sleep.

"Who is that?"

"It's Batya. She's very sick."

"I've had medical training. Let me see what I can do."

Reuven showed Eli the hole and he squeezed through, immediately turning his attention to Batya. He put his ear against her chest and checked the pulse in her neck.

"She's in serious shock," Eli said. "We should get her to the infirmary right away."

We left then, with Eli carrying Batya in his arms. Reuven and I, and his pretty dark-haired girlfriend, followed behind them.

chapter eighteen

We walked silently to the infirmary. I stayed well behind Eli so that there'd be no reason to talk to him.

He'd thought of me as just a little girl, a little girl with a big voice. The kiss had meant nothing to him.

His girlfriend was beautiful. She tried to make conversation with us, asking where we'd been and what had happened.

"It's too much to talk about right now," I said. I didn't want to talk to her, either.

When we reached the infirmary, the nurse rushed Batya inside.

"Will she be all right?" I asked.

"We can't waste time answering questions."

"We carried her all the way. For three nights."

"We won't know anything until you leave and let us examine her."

Her tone was unnecessarily harsh. It felt like a slap.

"Thank you," Reuven said to Eli, who had now linked arms with the girl. "Thank you for helping us."

"I am just glad that you're all alive." He smiled directly at me. "Your singing has stayed with me all these weeks, Halina."

"I need to find Tante Rosa." I turned away.

"Please give her my sympathy," Eli said. "About Grolsky."

And then I remembered, Tante Rosa and Mr. Grolsky were close. I wanted Tante Rosa to comfort me, but she needed to be comforted too. I wondered if she'd planned to leave with him. She'd always cautioned him and taken Mr. Moskin's side. But what did she think of the commander now?

"What will we say to Tante Rosa?" I asked Reuven when Eli was gone.

"I don't know," Reuven said. "Maybe we should just wait and let her tell us what happened."

But that didn't seem right. None of it did. I wondered if we should leave: Reuven, Tante Rosa, and I—and the girls, and Batya when she was well enough. I didn't want to be in the camp anymore. Not with a nurse who yelled at me for caring about my friend. Not with a leader who shot his own people. Not with Eli.

I hesitated when I came to the entrance to our *ziemlanka*, but when Tante Rosa saw us, she gathered me into her warm, fleshy arms. Both of us broke into sobs.

Tante Rosa smoothed my knotted hair. "It's a miracle you're alive!" The little girls crowded around us, tugging to break into the hug.

"What happened?" D'vora asked. "Why didn't you come back with the others?"

"Shah. You don't have to tell. It's over now. You're safe."

I looked over at Reuven, who was standing awkwardly beside us. "Reuven saved us," I said. "He insisted on waiting, just in case we came back. And then he insisted that we try to rescue Batya, and we did. He carried her all the way back, but she's very ill. They wouldn't tell us anything at the infirmary."

"See," Tante Rosa said, "I told you we needed you." She drew him close to her and kissed him on both cheeks. "Now, you should rest."

After the hard, cold ground, the straw on my bunk in the *ziemlanka* seemed like a bed I'd find in a palace. I lay down and listened to Reuven's light snores on the other side of the dugout. I wished he were closer. I'd felt safe with him beside me.

I tossed and turned, and tossed some more. Then I heard someone calling me from outside the *ziemlanka*.

"Halina! I need to talk to you!"

There was no mistaking Eli's smooth, melodious voice.

But I didn't want to see him. I turned my face into my arm.

"Halina . . ." The voice became louder. Reuven twisted and groaned in his sleep.

"Halina!"

Reuven groaned again.

"Shh . . . I'm coming."

He was standing outside against a tree, his violin tucked under his arm. The sun shone in his red hair, and he smiled broadly when he saw me, then raised his violin and broke into the first few notes of "The Russian Waltz," closing his eyes as if he were totally one with the music. Each note sung under his vibrato; the violin shivered with sadness as he slowly eased his bow along the strings, keeping the notes soft, yet drawing out every sound.

"I shouldn't be playing," he said. "The Germans are too close. But I couldn't resist."

I looked at the ground, which was covered with pine needles.

"Will you come for a walk with me?" he said. "There's a beautiful place I'd like to show you. It's quiet there, and I have something important to tell you."

"I don't think so."

"Please!" He touched my shoulders and made me look at him, an urgency in his blue eyes that I couldn't resist. "Hear me out before you judge me!"

We walked in silence. I could hear birds and the

high-pitched whine of mosquitoes. I was surprised to find myself following him down a familiar path, past the berry bushes and the large maple with peeling bark and fungi, past the thin white birches and the rock boulder, up the hill to my rock, and the space between the trees that faced the open sky.

Eli scrambled up and motioned me to join him. I sat next to him, but looked down at the moss. "I know this place," I said. "It's where I come when I want to be alone."

"Yes, and someone keeps leaving stones here. Look, they've spread nearly halfway around the rock!"

"Those are mine." It felt childish to admit it, but it didn't matter anymore. He thought of me as a child; I might as well be one.

"You have good taste in stones." He squeezed my hand, then reached over and turned my chin toward his face.

"Please look at me. I need to talk to you because I have something very important to do. And before I do it, I need to say that I didn't mean to mislead you. You're a beautiful, young girl with a great gift, but you're only fifteen. Raisl has been my girlfriend for a long time. I didn't mean to hurt your feelings. I just got carried away when I heard you sing."

I didn't answer him. I looked down at the rock. The moss blurred in front of me.

"I leave tonight for an important assignment. It's very

dangerous, so I have to say this to you now, because there may not be another chance."

"What are you talking about?"

"I can't say anything more. Please, give me your forgiveness now, because who knows if any of us will see another Yom Kippur." He gazed at me, a serious and somber look in his intense blue eyes, and this time I had to look back as his eyes fixed on mine.

"This is the most difficult thing we've attempted. I've probably already said too much. But I don't want to leave this incident hanging over us."

"Why would they ask you to do something so dangerous?"

He was silent for a minute. "I shouldn't be telling you this," he said. "I really shouldn't tell you anything. But trust me, when I say it's the only way. There's no other choice. You never told me what happened to you," he said, quickly changing the subject. "Unless you don't want to talk about it."

But I did want to tell. I ached to tell, and soon I was well into the story in all its excruciating and awful detail. Eli listened quietly. He took my hand, but I knew he meant only to comfort me. When I finished, we sat in the silence, watching the bright blue sky and listening to the faint breeze ruffle the birches beside us.

"You are so brave," he said. "I'll remember your bravery when I go on my mission tonight. I'll let it inspire me to do what must be done. I should go now and get ready. We leave as soon as it gets dark. But first, I want you to have this."

"What?"

I couldn't believe he was holding the violin and bow out to me.

"In case I don't come back . . . or don't come back right away," he added quickly. "Will you keep this for me?"

"Eli . . . I . . ."

"You're the only one I want to give this to. Even if you can't play. Perhaps after the war is over, you'll take lessons. Please . . ."

He grasped the violin by the neck and held it out to me.

"Where is the case?"

"I need the case," he said. "Find something in which to wrap it."

"All our clothing has lice. Nothing will be safe."

"Do the best you can." He ran his finger along the wood. "I'm amazed that none of the strings have broken. It must be a sign. I need to go now. Please say you'll forgive me."

I hesitated, and continued to fix my gaze on the moss. "I forgive you," I finally said. My voice was flat, but it was the best I could do.

"Thank you. Please, take care of my violin for me. Oh, I almost forgot. Here." He reached into his pocket and handed me a small packet. "It's rosin, for the bow," he explained. "In case you ever learn to play. It's a blessing to know that my violin is in your hands."

"But you'll come back."

"Of course I'll come back. I'm just a worrier sometimes. Keep this for me until I do come back. I look forward to the day when I can play it freely."

I watched him walk away until he disappeared into the curve of the birch trees. Despite everything, I still wanted to hold on to this moment. I ran my hands over the smooth wood of the violin, then put it under my neck. It was deceptively light, but awkward and bulky. I tried to move the bow along an open string, but the sound I made was so screechy that I quickly stopped. Carefully I cradled the instrument under my arm and started back to the *ziemlanka*.

I walked on a different path this time, figuring I could pass the infirmary and check on Batya. I wasn't surprised to see Reuven there, standing outside the camouflaged door.

"What's that?" he asked.

"Eli's violin."

"What are you doing with it?"

"He's going on some kind of mission and asked me to keep it for him until he gets back."

Reuven frowned. "I don't remember any talk of a mission."

"We haven't been here to hear about it," I said. But Reuven's words made me feel more uneasy, especially when I remembered what had happened to Mr. Grolsky. I didn't think Eli would do anything without Mr. Moskin's consent, but I didn't really know him that well.

"Have you asked the nurse anything?"

"I just got here. Let's go in together."

We ventured down the passage but were stopped quickly in the entryway.

"We still can't let you see her." It was a different nurse who stopped us—a young woman in our *ziemlanka* named Eva. "The risk of further infection is too great."

"What do you mean?" Reuven asked.

"She has a high fever. And she's lost a lot of blood. We're trying to keep her as comfortable as possible."

"What are you saying? Can't you tell us anything more?" Reuven sounded angry again. I touched his arm to calm him.

"I'm not saying anything. Just that she can't be exposed to more germs right now."

"But is she conscious?" I asked.

"Most of the time."

"That must mean she's getting better," Reuven said.

"She slips in and out of it, but she cries out so loudly that she disturbs the other patients. We had to give her something to help her sleep more peacefully."

"Please," I said, "let us see her. She's probably scared because she doesn't know where she is. Maybe if she sees us, she'll realize that she's safe."

"Not tonight." Eva was firm. "Perhaps tomorrow, if her fever goes down and she has a good night. Come back in the morning."

"Could we see Mr. Grolsky, then?" Reuven asked.

"Mr. Grolsky is not allowed to have visitors."

"If Batya wakes, tell her Halina and Reuven came to see her," I said. "Tell her we love her."

Eva smiled. "I will," she said. Then she retreated back into the dugout.

I sank down onto the ground, covering my face with my hands. Why should I be alive if Batya was going to die? Batya was the better, braver girl of the two of us. And Batya had absolute faith in God while I still wasn't sure if I believed in God or not. Nothing made sense. Nothing had order to it anymore. Perhaps that was why I'd felt the way I did about Eli. It was really about the way he played the violin, a small slice of beauty in a heartless world. I understood now why he'd kissed me after my singing, and I could forgive him, really forgive him. It wasn't about romance, just connection. Because there had to be something that made you want to survive, something that kept you going after everyone you loved had been slaughtered.

"Ready to go?" I felt Reuven's shy touch on my shoulder.

"Let's not go back just yet."

"We have to believe that Batya will be all right," Reuven said. "She will be. I'm sure of it. She's like a cat with nine lives. She won't give up. I know she won't."

"We'll come back tomorrow," I said, "as soon as the sun rises."

chapter
nineteen

When I got back to the *ziemlanka*, I wrapped the violin and bow in Mama's coat, then tried to figure out the best place to put it. There were no shelves other than the sleeping areas, and the girls often climbed around without noticing what was there. After pondering for a while, I tucked the violin into the farthest corner of the hut and put my ruined boots in front of it as a barrier. Once I had time to tell everyone that the violin was there, we could make a safer place for it.

That night I slept in fits and snatches, waiting for dawn so I could go and see Batya. At the sound of each loud breeze I woke up and squinted in the darkness, trying to discern any crack of light shining through the dugout, but each time it was still dark. I closed my eyes and tried to sleep more deeply.

Faces floated before me—Mama at the edge of the pit, Batya pale and slumped over Reuven's shoulder, Eli saying good-bye with worry in his face, the German soldier . . . I shut my eyes more tightly, determined to sleep, forcing myself to think of more pleasant thoughts, . . . going to see *The Magic Flute* in Berlin, being at the beach with Mama, running down a large sand-covered dune into the ocean . . .

The noise at first sounded like the crashing of large waves. I was little again, running to the safety of the shore as fast as I could, back to Mama—and some man. Georg? No, this was before Georg. I wasn't sure who it was. The face was shadowy, insignificant.

Then Tante Rosa was shaking me. "We have to move right now. The Germans are attacking."

I opened my eyes. The sound I'd heard was not waves crashing, but gunfire.

"The men are fighting them," Tante Rosa said. "Moskin has ordered the women and children to head deeper into the forest."

"What about Batya?"

"We must be ready in five minutes. Take only what you can carry."

"But who will carry Batya?"

"The infirmary is well hidden. The sick will join us later, after the fighting is over. If they come now, they will slow us down. We need to get as many people to safety as quickly as possible."

"But if the Germans find Batya? What . . . ?"

"Shah," Tante Rosa said. "Moskin has put me in charge of the women and children in this unit. You must listen to me."

I didn't want to listen. I wanted to find Reuven. Together we could carry Batya. We'd carried her so far already, this small trip would be nothing. But I got up and began to gather my things.

"Where's Reuven?"

"All the men are gone," Tante Rosa said. "The commander asked every boy over twelve to help fight."

I put on my clothes, layering two dresses on top of each other, with my slacks underneath them, then reached for Mama's coat, gasping when I heard something crash.

Eli's violin.

I grabbed a pine bough and lit it, afraid to look.

The violin was intact, though the bridge had fallen from beneath the strings. Someone would be able to repair it. I felt around the floor for the small piece of wood, but I couldn't find it anywhere.

"Halina! Come! Everyone else has left! We must be at the gathering spot in ten minutes!"

"I've lost the bridge to Eli's violin."

"That should be the worst thing that happens to us! Come!"

I felt around the rucksack before I put the violin inside, making sure there was nothing there that would scratch it. I pulled out the lucky stone and put it in Mama's coat pocket. Then I gathered Batya's special things. Her brass candlesticks had been given to the commander, but she still had her father's *tallis* and *tefillin*. I wrapped the violin in the *tallis*, and put Mama's handkerchief against my father's picture for extra cushioning so the frame wouldn't rub against the violin. I put on Mama's coat and my ruined boots and crept out of the dugout.

Even though I'd heard shooting many times, it had never been so fast and furious. The shots came from all over. Each blast followed the next, with no pause in between.

"Come!" Tante Rosa grabbed my wrist, leading me to a small clearing at the edge of the marsh, where approximately thirty people stood in the darkness, many of them mothers trying to hush their crying children.

"We need order!" Tante Rosa raised her voice above the others. "The swamp is waist-deep, and it's easy to sink even farther. We will tie ropes around ourselves to make sure we stay together. Small children must be carried."

"Can't we go around it?" someone asked. "We'll ruin everything we have."

"It will take too long. Moskin gave explicit orders. The

Russian Army is on the other side and they will protect us, if we can get to them. We need to divide into small groups—four women plus two children in a group. That way we can take turns carrying the children, and everyone will have someone to look out for."

The women began to tie themselves together with ropes. I inched away from their dim spots of light, my own light pointed behind me so no one could see me. From the shelter of a thick tree trunk I waited until I heard splashes of water, children whimpering and mothers shushing them. Then I turned and ran as fast as I could to the infirmary.

I would not leave without Batya.

Eva was still standing guard, but I ignored her and rushed in as if I belonged there, trying to find Batya in the scant light.

"What are you doing here?" Eva whispered sharply. "You're risking everything! The Germans might have seen you!"

"I won't leave the camp without Batya," I said. "I can't."

Eva sighed. "Well, if you're going to stay, you may as well—"

A blast of gunfire interrupted the rest of the sentence. She grabbed me and we hunkered down on the floor, listening to torrents of bullets that sliced the air around us.

In her sleep, Batya moaned.

"Shh, it's all right," I whispered. From my spot on the floor I reached up and squeezed her hand. "Sleep," I whispered. "It's just a bad dream."

"A visit from the *Shechinah*," Batya mumbled, her hand dropping from mine.

Another blast of gunfire followed.

"We're doomed!" I heard Mr. Grolsky's voice in the darkness. "Just as I predicted, the Germans have come! Moskin is an idiot!"

"Shah!" Eva whispered angrily. "Why don't you shout louder and tell the Germans exactly where we are!"

We waited there on the ground. The gunfire lessened for a while, then increased again. I heard German voices right outside the *ziemlanka*. Then a loud blast. Then more fighting, and then the noise seemed to subside; the battle became more distant. I helped Eva soothe Batya's hot body with cold compresses and dress Mr. Grolsky's wound. I made hot tea and gruel. Suddenly the gunfire stopped. There was silence, an eerie, stark quiet. I wondered if we were the only ones left in the whole encampment.

"If it's dark, we should get out of here," Mr. Grolsky said. "Before they come back."

"We can't move the little girl."

"I'll carry her," Mr. Grolsky said.

"You can't even walk yourself!"

"Give me some sticks for crutches and I'll drag the leg."

"I can carry Batya," I said. "But is it really safe to leave?"

"There haven't been any shots for a while," Mr. Grolsky

explained. "I know how the Germans work. They've done what they need to do and gone off. They'll come back later to reap the spoils."

We got ready. Outside, the woods smelled like fire and death. I took out a match to light my pine branch. Mr. Grolsky stopped me.

"It's too dangerous to use lights," he said. "But I know this area like the back of my hand. We'll use this rope to keep us together. I'll tie it to my crutch and you hold on to it."

Eva carried my rucksack along with her own. I tied the sleeves of Mama's coat around my waist, and used it as a sling to carry Batya. We walked as quickly as we could, but Mr. Grolsky struggled with the crutches. Random spurts of gunfire pierced the silence. Finally we made it to the edge of the swamp, where we stopped and tied the rope around our waists to make sure we'd stay together.

I stepped forward and put a toe into the muck. Batya's arms encircled my neck; her legs dangled on either side of my hip in the makeshift sling. Mr. Grolsky cursed as he tried to drag his crutches out of the sinking mass. Finally he gave up, handed his crutches to Eva, and crawled on his knees.

Every step was difficult. The swamp seemed to last forever. After several hours we tied ourselves to a group of trees in the mud so we could rest without sinking. Eva gave us some pieces of dried meat for energy, but even they were covered with mud.

My rucksack was splattered with it, and I feared for the violin, which made me think of Eli. Was he safe? And what about Reuven? We could still hear gunfire in the distance, so Mr. Grolsky didn't let us rest for long. My shoulders ached as I lifted Batya onto my back again. The water became too deep for Mr. Grolsky to use his hands to guide him; he had to walk on his knees alone. Water spilled into the tops of my boots, making it even harder to lift each foot out of the mud. Each step splattered us with its smell of dead things. Batya moaned.

"Shh! It will be all right." I reached into Mama's coat pocket to squeeze the lucky stone.

It was gone!

I reached into the pocket again. I had placed everything else in the rucksack to keep it safe. Why had I put the stone in my pocket? I checked the other side. Nothing. It had floated away somewhere and disappeared into the mud of the swamp with all the dead things.

It couldn't be. I reached into both pockets again. The wool was wet and soggy. In desperation I swept at the water with my hand, but of course, stones sink to the bottom.

I bit my lip. It was only superstition, I told myself. No more real than God might be. I'd have to depend on myself, on my will to stay alive, and to save Batya.

The water began to recede, quickly going from thigh-high to knee-high, to ankle-deep. The mud was less sticky on this side of the swamp, and Mr. Grolsky was able to use his crutches and go more quickly. The gunfire seemed to subside. Could we really be safe now? We crossed the last few meters of the swamp and stepped up into the muddy footprints of those who had gone before us. We'd done it! I'd carried Batya across the swamp. She no longer even felt heavy. I walked faster, humming the aria of the Queen of the Night as softly as I could, though it kept wanting to burst out of me. The sky lightened and a sliver of sun warmed the damp and foggy haze.

A group of men headed toward us, wearing the hammer-and-sickle insignia of the Russian Army.

"We're almost there," I said to Batya, though I wasn't sure she was even awake.

"*Brukhim haboim.* Welcome, friends!"

I was surprised to hear Yiddish spoken in a familiar Polish accent, and even more astounded when I looked up and recognized the face of the man who had greeted us.

chapter
twenty

Georg Goldmann extended his hand to Mr. Grolsky. "In the name of the Russian Army, we welcome you." His voice was more hoarse and reedy than ever, his face was thinner with a gray stubble of beard, but the man was clearly Georg. He greeted Eva. Then he moved on to me. I was still carrying Batya, and my face was partially hidden. "Is there a problem?" he asked. "Lay her down and let me look."

Batya looked different in her illness, thinner and more pale. I may have looked different too, though I didn't think so, just dirtier and more unkempt. But Georg glanced from Batya to me several times before he recognized us. Then he broke into a broad smile.

"Halina?"

His long spiderlike arms enveloped me in a hug; his touch was firm and warm, though he still smelled of garlic.

"I prayed every night that you were safe," he said. "So many people were shot by the Nazis once they broke through the tunnel. I prayed you weren't one of them. I promised your mother that if anything happened to her, I would take care of you. I hope she is looking down on us, watching this moment."

I didn't reply, but I didn't let go of him either, nor did he let go of me. I let him hug me the way I'd wanted Mama to hug me the day we'd separated at the ghetto gate.

"This is Batya Rojak, isn't it?" he asked. "Come, let's get her to our medical people."

He took Batya in his arms and we walked for another half-hour to a group of makeshift tents in a thick grove of evergreens.

Tante Rosa came rushing up to us. "Halina, you're safe!" she cried as she fell into Mr. Grolsky's arms. "Yitzhak, how did you ever manage?"

I followed Georg as he took Batya to the medic. "We're safe," I whispered. She didn't respond. She was sleeping—or unconscious. I wasn't sure which.

"Will she be all right?" I asked.

Georg had to translate my question into Russian.

"He says to come back later, after he's had a chance to examine her."

I didn't want to leave, but Georg led me away, his firm arm around my shoulder. "This is Halina, *meyn takhter*," he announced.

There was a murmuring that spread among the crowd and echoes of "*takhter*," the Yiddish word for "daughter."

He's not my father! I wanted to shout. My father was the picture in my rucksack, Grisha, whoever he had been.

But was Georg being my father any more preposterous than Batya being my sister, and Reuven being . . . I wasn't sure what to think of Reuven, other than that he clearly loved me enough to risk his life and wait for me in the barn, as Georg also had once risked his life for my safety. Why shouldn't they be my family?

We sat by a fire and shared a small meal. After we ate, Tante Rosa led me to my sleeping quarters, a large piece of canvas propped up by sticks. Tante Rosa said we would set up a new site here, but it would take a while to dig *ziemlankas*. For now, the women were sleeping in makeshift tents, the men out in the open.

"Shayna and D'vora want to sleep with you," Tante Rosa said.

The little girls were already curled up together on a torn blanket that was so thin I could see the rocks jutting out underneath it. But it didn't matter. I was safe—at least for now. I went into the tent and unpacked my rucksack. The violin was muddy, but it had survived the journey. Mama's handkerchief had also been splattered, but a good washing would get rid of most of the spots. I smoothed it out beside me, uncovering my father's strong and solid face.

I lay down beside Shayna and D'vora, listening to the rhythm of their sweet and peaceful breathing. It could be a song, I thought, as Shayna moaned and put her fat little arm around my neck. A simple song about breathing and surviving.

After I rested, Georg told me his story. "We kept planning escapes," he said. "Each night we'd arrange for more people to go through the tunnel, but then the Nazis started suspecting me and I had to escape too."

He'd been traveling in a small group, but soon lost track of the others when they heard shots and all ran for cover. He stayed hidden in a pile of cow dung until the gunfire stopped. Then he walked for days, tracking the sun in order to head east, toward the Russian Army. Several partisan units rejected him because he was a Jew and he didn't have a weapon. Finally he found a group that was willing to accept him.

I told Georg about how we got to the camp, how the scouts found Reuven and me in the barn after Batya had left with Reuven's brothers, how Batya had miraculously returned, but the brothers had not.

"And do you still love music? Have you had any moments where it's been safe enough to sing?"

"There was a boy at the camp who loved my singing. He

played the violin, but he had to go on a special mission, so he gave it to me for safekeeping until he returned."

Georg looked at me strangely. "I didn't see you carrying a violin."

"He didn't give me the case. He said he needed it!"

"Then he was the one!" Georg took my hand. "I hope to God things didn't turn out as badly as I fear they did."

"What are you talking about?"

"We gave him the explosives," Georg said. "One of our men saw him in the village with the German soldiers. It was our plan. He was brave enough to carry it out."

"I don't understand!" I said, though my chest began to tighten.

"Your friend is a very smart boy. Very smart and very brave. He used his violin to befriend German soldiers, then duped them into giving him their secrets, which he told to us. But we gave him a choice in accepting this mission. Of course, he didn't hesitate for a moment. He was—he is—a true fighter."

"What mission? What did he do?"

"We filled his violin case with explosives," Georg said. "The German soldiers often gather in crowds to drink on Saturday nights. The bomb was set to go off at eleven P.M., when the crowd would be large. The hard part of the mission was to sneak out unnoticed as close to the explosion time as possible, because the Germans would know that a serious musician would never leave his violin unattended."

"And if he didn't?"

"He knew it might be impossible to get away without caus-ing suspicion and jeopardizing the mission."

"But what happened?"

"No one knows. But we had forewarning of the German attack on your camp. Your commander knew it was coming. We were expecting that this explosion would injure enough people and cause enough chaos to stave it off. Apparently that didn't happen. We made a mistake in not taking precautions. We should have evacuated the encampment, regardless."

It took me a moment to realize what Georg had said—or what he meant by what he hadn't said. An explosion may have gone off. Apparently it hadn't hurt the Germans enough to fore-stall their plans, but it may have hurt, it may have killed, Eli.

I sat silent, stupefied, the few lines I knew of that sad and soulful "Russian Waltz" playing over and over again in my head. The hopeful young couple remembering their first dance and the whole glittering future lying before them.

Georg touched my arm. "If he is dead, he will have died a hero's death."

I looked down at the grass, and at the crackling fire where a pot of soup was boiling. Eli knew, I thought. He knew when he begged me to take the violin that he wasn't likely to come back. I tried to be discreet as I wiped the tears from my cheek.

"He wasn't your boyfriend, was he?" Georg's voice was gentle.

I was tempted to tell him it was none of his business. And it wasn't. But I countered with a question of my own.

"Did you really love my mother?"

"It was dangerous to love anyone in those times, as it still is." Georg brought his hand to his face. "But I did love your mother. I wanted to marry her, but she worried that the responsibility of a wife and child would weigh me down. The Germans threatened family members as a way of forcing *Judenrat* officials to carry out their bidding. We agreed in the end that it was best perceived that I was unattached. That's why my visits were secret; that's why I ignored you when I saw you on the streets. Any attachment was dangerous. Any connection could be manipulated."

"Did she ever tell you anything about my father?"

Georg shook his head. "We didn't talk about the past. But she consistently entreated me to look out for you. Attachments are dangerous, but your mother loved you and she would have risked her life for you ten times over."

"My father was a peasant. That's all Mama would ever say about him. I have his blood. I'm strong and I'm good at working with my hands. That's why I've survived here."

"Perhaps, but you also have your mother's bravery and courage. You know, she helped us. She sewed bags to store the dirt we dug out of the tunnel; she helped people smuggle weapons and medicine out of the ghetto. She would have never told you, because it would have been too dangerous, but she was one of the many who made your escape possible. She smuggled in the engineers who helped us design the tunnel by pretending they were her lovers. She knew who the softhearted Germans were, the guards who'd let a smooching couple have a few minutes of happiness and not bother with papers. Even though she didn't want to leave the ghetto, she was willing to risk her life to help others who did want to escape. You should be proud of her."

"Mama was a spy?"

"She was a hero, Halina. Just like you. We all are heroes."

I was silent for a moment, thinking about what Georg had said, thinking about all the people I'd lost, especially Mama, and probably Eli, too. Would Batya recover? And Reuven? Where was Reuven?

"What happened to the men who were fighting?" I asked. "Has anyone heard?"

"No one knows," Georg said. "There are dead all over your encampment, Germans and Jews alike. A group of us is going back there as soon as the sun sets to see what we can find out and to help any of those who might be injured."

"Please look for Reuven. He and Batya are my best friends. And if you can, try to find out what happened to Eli."

"I will," he said. "I must go and get ready to leave. Wish me good luck." He extended his arms.

I wished I had my lucky stone or something to give him, but all I had was myself.

I hugged him despite his garlic smell and promised myself I wouldn't bristle the next time he called me "daughter."

chapter
twenty-one

Good news," Tante Rosa said to me the next day as I
was helping to dig *ziemlankas* for the new site. "They
just smuggled in a shipment of medicines. Batya is much better.
They expect her to make a full recovery."

I threw down my shovel and hugged her. "When can I see
Batya?"

"Tonight. And only for a short time. They want her to rest
a bit more first."

When I picked up the spade, it felt lighter. I felt so hopeful
suddenly, almost lucky. We'd been through so much and it
would all be worth it. Batya would be all right. Georg would
find Reuven—I felt sure of it. Maybe he'd even find Eli.

I began to sing. We were so deep into the forest, it was safer to sing more loudly here. I sang the first few lines of "The Russian Waltz" and the aria from the Queen of the Night. I sang Batya's prayer chants without words. All except *Kaddish*. I was determined not to give up hope.

That night I went to see Batya. She looked pale and weak, but she smiled and sat up when she saw me.

"We're safe," I said. "We're with the Russians."

"I know. That's why I can't understand what anyone says. At first I thought I was having more nightmares."

"Not nightmares," I said. "Visits from the *Shechinah*."

She smiled again and grasped my hand. "Did you really carry me through a swamp? And is Georg Goldmann really here?"

"Yes, it's really Georg."

"What a miracle!"

"Mr. Grolsky led us through the swamp. He had to use crutches. Sometimes he had to drag through the bottom on his hands and knees. I have your father's *tallis*. I used it to wrap Eli's violin. He . . ."

"What?"

I didn't want to upset her, or upset myself by telling her. I had to remember to be hopeful.

"Georg went to look for him." I chose my words carefully. "And Reuven, too. All the men and boys stayed behind to fight the Germans."

"I'll pray to *HaShem*," Batya said. "I'll pray that they're safe."

I went back to my tent, took out the violin, and looked at it for a long time. I stroked its smooth wood. It still smelled like swamp mud, but it had made the journey without a single scratch. If Eli didn't return, I'd keep the violin forever. I'd find a way to repair the bridge. Georg was right. Attachments were dangerous. But you needed to make them anyway, and then just hope for luck to save the people you loved.

But when night fell, I felt less lucky, less hopeful. I kept imagining Eli tortured by a mass of German soldiers, Reuven shot the way Mama had been shot, thoughtlessly and without remorse. I buried my head in the shirt I'd been using as a pillow, trying to stifle my sobs so Shayna and D'vora wouldn't hear me.

"Halina." I felt a hand on my back, on the part that ached, right between the shoulder blades. It was Tante Rosa.

"You can't spend time mourning the dead," she said. "The best gift you can give them is your own survival."

I sat up and looked at her. "If they were dead, I could mourn them. But I don't know if Reuven and Eli are dead or not. That's what makes it so hard. Sometimes I even think that Mama's alive, that she escaped from the pit, even though I know Batya saw her at the edge."

Tante Rosa took my hand between hers. "My husband was taken by the Germans and sent away," she said softly. "And I have no idea what happened to him. Sometimes when I see someone arriving with the scouts in the distance, I think it's him. I think I recognize his beard, or his build, or the shape of his face. But then the man gets closer and I realize that isn't him. It's like a little death each time, but you get used to it. That's why you can't think of the past so much. You have to hold on to a reason for living. Promise me that after the war is over, you'll study voice again and be a singer."

Yes, I thought. That is what I would do. I'd sing for Mama.

And for everyone else who'd been important to me and hadn't come back.

A week went by. Georg did not appear. Neither did anyone else from the encampment. Each day Batya got stronger. That was the only consolation. After a few days she was released from the infirmary. She slept with the girls and me in our little tent and helped gather firewood while I dug *ziemlankas*. In the mornings and evenings she still chanted her prayers. I asked her to teach me the words.

One night a group led by Mr. Moskin's brother came back, but Reuven, Eli, and Georg were not among them. They told us the Germans had retreated. There were casualties, but everyone left was preparing to evacuate the camp and come here. Mr. Moskin's brother told us we would set this camp up differently. We would have a central kitchen, and a row of huts to serve as workshops—tailoring, gun repair, a smithy, even a tannery. We would keep livestock and more horses. We were deep into the forest now, with few roads and Russian partisan groups all around us.

It would be safer to be out in the open, to make more noise. The tide of the war was beginning to turn too. The Russians were beating back the Germans in the forests, and the Allies had begun to win battles in the west. I found out that Georg was still at the encampment, making inquiries about the missing. I couldn't bear to ask directly about Reuven or Eli. As long as I didn't know, I could still hope. I sang the next morning as I chopped wood for the huts. I sang because it was the only thing no one could ever take away from me. I had to go on, even if Reuven and Eli were dead, even if Mama really wasn't coming back.

"I'm amazed at how much wood you've chopped," Tante Rosa said to me. "You're so strong!"

"I'm built like my father," I said. "I never knew him, but I think I have his peasant blood." I had Mama's bravery too, I remembered, and something from each of my friends: Eli's passion for music, Reuven's loyalty and persistence, Batya's—would I ever have Batya's unquestioned faith, her ability to see good where there was no good, her spunky bravery and willingness to speak up?

"Look," Tante Rosa shouted. "There's a group coming back!"

I wondered as I scanned the line whether Tante Rosa was also looking for her husband. I wondered if she ever stopped hoping for a miracle. But I only wondered this for a second, because there was Reuven making his way to the head of the line, a broad smile on his face. Batya, who was standing nearby, broke into a run and I followed. Soon the three of us were

locked in an embrace. Huddled together, we waited for everyone else to walk by until we were alone.

"*Baruch HaShem*," Batya whispered.

We held on to each other for a long, long time. "Welcome
home," I said.

"I worried about you so much," Reuven said. "Georg told
me Batya was still very ill when he left. I was so glad to see both
of you running toward me."

"Where is Georg? And what about Eli?" I couldn't help
but ask.

Reuven was silent. I felt myself start to shake.

"Georg's coming back with the last group tomorrow,"
Reuven finally said. "He spent days looking for Eli; he even
risked his life going into the town at night, but none of the
people in the safe houses had any information about him. We
don't know for sure, but it's likely that he's dead."

I sat down, feeling too heavy to stand. I hardly knew Eli, really.
His death was a small thing compared to Mama's, and I should be
happy enough just to see Reuven alive. But I couldn't be.

"We can say *Kaddish*," Batya said.

I nodded, though saying *Kaddish* didn't seem like enough.
But I could keep my promise to Tante Rosa to sing. And perhaps I could learn to play Eli's violin and let it sing with me.

"We lost many people in the fighting," Reuven said. "But we
finally drove out the Nazis. I shot a soldier who was trying to

enter the infirmary. I planted myself there to make sure that nothing would happen to Batya."

"I was in the infirmary too," I said. "I wouldn't leave without Batya. We crossed the swamp with Mr. Grolsky after the battle."

Reuven reached into his pocket. "I wondered about that. Then this is yours."

I saw a glint of gold as he held out his hand.

"I can't believe it!"

"It brought me luck."

"No, you brought your own luck." I touched the stone. "I don't need this anymore."

"But you should keep it," Batya said. "Because we don't have a lot to hold on to."

She was right. I had Mama's coat and handkerchief, my father's picture, Eli's violin, and my lucky stone. That was all.

I put the stone in my pocket. "It will have to be enough then."

"*Dayenu.*" Batya smiled.

It wasn't enough. We both knew that. Reuven, too. But we had one another. I had Tante Rosa and the girls—and Georg, the closest I'd ever had to a father. I had my strength, my memories, and my singing.

Dayenu. It would have to be enough.

afterword

I was first inspired to write this story when reading about
Tuvia Bielski at the National Museum of the Holocaust in
Washington, D.C. With his brothers, Bielski organized a net-
work of encampments in the forests of western Belorussia that
offered protection to over 1,200 Jewish men, women, and children who were able to escape from the ghettos. While most
partisan units were solely concerned with guerrilla fighting and
only accepted men, Bielski's primary mission was not to recruit
fighters, but to save as many Jews as possible. Any Jew, regardless of age, gender, or state of health was welcome into the
Bielski encampment.

Though there was only a paragraph at the museum men-
tioning Bielski among the many unsung heroes of the
Holocaust, the story intrigued me. What would it be like to live
in the forests for months or years under the threat of attack? I

began to find out what I could. Many sources were helpful, but all were scanty. However, Nechama Tec's excellent book, *Defiance: The Story of the Bielski Partisans*, gave a detailed account of the history of the Bielski encampment and the trials and tribulations of daily life.

I tried to be as true as possible to settings and daily activities, and to incorporate historical events I read about, though not necessarily in the context in which they happened. For example, there was an escape tunnel constructed in the Norwogrodek ghetto. The Germans did engage in a direct attack on the partisans and the camp was forced to move across the swamp deeper into the Belorussian forests. There was also a historical reference to a Jewish boy who befriended the Germans through his music and later duped them by filling his violin case with explosives. In that case, the bomb did go off.

The story itself and the characters are all fictional. I had no intention of mirroring Bielski in my portrayal of Moskin or basing any other character on people I'd read about. My goal was not to relate history as much as to explore the timeless issues of love, faith, and loss as they relate to Halina's story.

Like Halina, my journey of writing this book depended on the encouragement, insight, and support of others. Thanks first to the National Yiddish Book Center for supplying correct transliterated spellings, to Miriam Leader of the Hot Kishkes Klezmer Band for the translation of the lyrics to "The Russian

Waltz" (also commonly known as "The Expectation Waltz"), and to Gregory William Frux for his knowledge and guidance in researching the topography of the Polish and Belorussian forests. Thanks to my photographer, Andrew Morris-Friedman, and to my agent, Alison Picard. My editor, Alexandra Cooper, whose astute feedback helped me bring this story to an even deeper place, deserves particular acknowledgment. Additional thanks to members of my family who read and gave feedback on earlier drafts: Shel Horowitz, Alana Horowitz Friedman, Rafael Horowitz Friedman, Susan Friedman, and Stanley Friedman.

And special thanks to Jeannine Atkins, Bruce Carson, and Lisa Kleinholz, who cheerfully read the rough beginnings and helped me navigate my way out of several dead-end drafts to find the true path to the story. You are the best writing colleagues one could ever hope for. With you alone, *Dayenu*.